W9-BSI-666

The
Fox Hunt Mystery

Nancy hunched down over Hopscotch's neck as she galloped across the meadow. Laura streaked past on Morning Glory. The black horse raised his head, anticipating the jump about twenty yards away.

Suddenly, Mr. Hathaway, Mrs. Passano, and the riders close behind them veered to the side.

"Stop!" Mrs. Passano shouted. "Don't jump!"

Across the top of the fence ahead, someone had strung barbed wire. Its sharp points glinted menacingly in the bright autumn sunshine.

Nancy instantly pulled on the reins and sat deep in the saddle. Any horse that jumped over the barbed wire was sure to be seriously injured!

Nancy Drew
Mystery Stories

Available from MINSTREL Books

For orders other than by individual consumers, Pocket Books
grants a discount on the purchase of **10 or more** copies of
single titles for special markets or premium use. For further
details, please write to the Vice-President of Special Markets,
Pocket Books, 1633 Broadway, New York, NY 10019-6785,
8th Floor.

For information on how individual consumers can place
orders, please write to Mail Order Department, Simon &
Schuster Inc., 200 Old Tappan Road, Old Tappan, NJ 07675.

NANCY DREW® 132

THE FOX HUNT MYSTERY

CAROLYN KEENE

A MINSTREL® BOOK

Published by POCKET BOOKS

New York   London   Toronto   Sydney   Tokyo   Singapore

The sale of this book without its cover is unauthorized. If you purchased this book without a cover, you should be aware that it was reported to the publisher as "unsold and destroyed." Neither the author nor the publisher has received payment for the sale of this "stripped book."

This book is a work of fiction. Names, characters, places and incidents are products of the author's imagination or are used fictitiously. Any resemblance to actual events or locales or persons, living or dead, is entirely coincidental.

A MINSTREL PAPERBACK *Original*

 A Minstrel Book published by
POCKET BOOKS, a division of Simon & Schuster Inc.
1230 Avenue of the Americas, New York, NY 10020

Copyright © 1996 by Simon & Schuster Inc.
Produced by Mega-Books, Inc.

All rights reserved, including the right to reproduce this book or portions thereof in any form whatsoever. For information address Pocket Books, 1230 Avenue of the Americas, New York, NY 10020

ISBN: 0-671-50510-6

First Minstrel Books printing August 1996

10 9 8 7 6 5 4 3

NANCY DREW, NANCY DREW MYSTERY STORIES, A MINSTREL BOOK and colophon are registered trademarks of Simon & Schuster Inc.

Cover art by Craig Nelson

Printed in the U.S.A.

Contents

1

Sky Meadow Farm

"I bet that jump's three feet tall!" George Fayne exclaimed, pointing to a large post-and-rail fence in the middle of the outdoor riding ring. She flashed Nancy Drew a challenging look. "Think you can get Hopscotch over it?"

"Let's see," Nancy replied, her blue eyes sparkling. Turning toward the fence, she urged on the glossy bay mare, her adrenaline pumping as she saw the fence looming ahead. Hopscotch lifted off the ground, and Nancy leaned forward, taking the fence with ease. Exhilarated, she guided Hopscotch to the side of the ring. "Made it! Your turn, George."

"I was afraid you'd say that," George said, and grinned. "Oh, well, here goes."

Nancy watched George sail over the fence on the horse she was riding, a coppery chestnut gelding named Lancelot. At the other end of the ring, their friend Laura Passano cantered on Morning Glory, the largest and friskiest horse of the three.

"Wow!" George said as she pulled up next to Nancy. "I'd forgotten how much fun riding can be."

Tucking a lock of her reddish blond hair back up under her helmet, eighteen-year-old Nancy glanced over at her friend. Dark-haired George loved sports and outdoor activities. She was the perfect guest at a horse farm, Nancy thought.

"I'm glad we decided to take Laura up on her invitation," George said. "I just hope we can relax and ride horses—*not* solve another mystery."

Nancy chuckled, then made a face. "Solving a mystery is the last thing on my mind," she promised.

Nancy had earned quite a reputation as a detective in her hometown of River Heights. Wherever she went, she always seemed to land in the middle of a mystery, as both she and George knew only too well.

"You guys hungry?" Laura asked as she rode over to Nancy and George. "I think it's about time for dinner." She stroked Morning Glory's soft black mane as he pawed the ground. "Let's go in. I can tell the horses are hungry, too," she added.

"Now that you mention it," George said, her eyes lighting up, "I'm starved."

Nancy glanced down the hill to the barn, a large red building with a pitched roof. Surrounding it was a lush pasture, where five or six horses grazed calmly on the dark green grass.

"Hopscotch is the best," Nancy said to Laura as they started back to the stable. She patted the mare's silky neck.

"I thought you two would get along," Laura said brightly. "And how did you like Lancelot, George?"

"He's beautiful, and he's easy to ride," George said. "Everything about this afternoon has been perfect. It's just too bad Bess couldn't come." George's cousin, Bess Marvin, was Nancy's other best friend.

"Well, Bess couldn't miss the benefit party for the River Heights Children's Museum," Nancy pointed out. "Especially considering that she and her mom organized the whole thing."

"I guess she's excused, then," Laura joked.

Laura hadn't changed much since Nancy had last seen her, two summers ago, when the Passanos came to River Heights to visit Laura's aunt. She was still sweet and friendly, Nancy thought. When Laura had written to invite Nancy and her friends to visit the Passanos' horse farm in Maryland, the River Heights girls eagerly accepted. Nancy and George had arrived that day, and Laura immediately took them riding.

Outside the barn door, the three girls dismounted, and Laura gave Morning Glory an affectionate hug.

"Was Morning Glory born here at Sky Meadow Farm?" Nancy asked, admiring the horse's gorgeous pitch-black coat, broken only by the white star on his forehead and his two white socks. His dark eyes looked alert as he held his head up proudly.

"We *do* breed horses for hunting and showing," Laura replied. "But our foals are still too young for me to ride. And my old horse, Dundee, isn't up to going on long fox hunts anymore. One day I saw Morning Glory at a breeder's in the area, and I fell in love with him. Unfortunately, everyone else around here wanted him, too. My dad and I outbid everyone and won him last spring in an auction—it was pretty fierce." Laura paused, then frowned. For a split second, Nancy thought Laura seemed troubled.

"What happened?" Nancy asked.

Laura shook her head quickly. "Another girl, Alexa Shaw, wanted Morning Glory, too," she explained. "She's barely spoken to me since."

"Who's Alexa Shaw?" George asked.

"A girl I graduated from high school with," Laura explained. "Her mother and my mom are best friends. Mrs. Shaw's nice, but Alexa's nothing but trouble. She's really pretty and totally spoiled. All our lives, our mothers tried to push us together, hoping we'd be friends. They shouldn't have bothered. But I do feel sorry for her—her father died last year in a riding accident."

Just then a short, small man with tousled gray hair and bright blue eyes approached the girls. With his hunched shoulders and leathery face, Nancy thought he looked like someone out of a fairy tale—a leprechaun, maybe.

"Can I help you, girls?" the man asked, setting down a bucket of water. "Let me take the horses from you."

"Oh, yes, Peter, thanks," Laura said, handing Morning Glory's reins to him. "I'll help you in a few minutes." Laura introduced the girls to Peter Greenbriar, the groom at Sky Meadow.

He hurried to take the reins from Nancy and George. "I see you've been using the curb bit on Lancelot's bridle lately, Miss Laura," he commented in a thin, nasal voice. "That's good. With his tough mouth, he needs a strong bit."

"I'm pretty careful about Lancelot's bit," Laura assured him.

"Peter's a great help to my mother and me," Laura explained as the groom led the three horses away. "We have a dozen horses at the stable. We'd never be able to take care of them without him. And Dad doesn't get involved in the hands-on care of the horses. He handles the business side of the farm."

"Can we have a tour of the stable?" George asked.

Laura looked at her watch. "As long as it's quick," she said. "I like to cool down Morning Glory myself."

Inside the stable door, which slid open sideways, Nancy found herself standing in a large center aisle. Twelve stalls ran the length of it. Nancy could see horses bobbing their heads over their half-doors. Only a few stalls were empty. On the opposite side was a tack room, where the saddles and bridles were stored, as well as a feed room, an office, and a few more stalls. Nancy sniffed. The stable had a pungent, musty smell of hay and leather.

"Here's a sweet-looking horse," Nancy said, stopping beside a dappled gray mare with soft brown eyes. The mare nuzzled her gently.

"This is Dundee," Laura explained. "She's part Arabian—that's why her face is slightly scooped. She's a bit too old to hunt or show, so we use her for breeding. She gave birth to an adorable foal last spring."

Nancy and George reached over Dundee's stall door to pat her neck.

Laura glanced at her watch again. "Wow, it's six o'clock already, and dinner's at seven. Why don't you guys go back to the house to change, while I take care of Morning Glory?"

After giving Dundee one last pat, Nancy and George walked back to the Passanos' home, an old stone farmhouse surrounded by large oaks and maples. Nancy and George entered through the kitchen.

Mrs. Passano, who had not been home when the girls arrived, was in the kitchen, cutting up vegetables. "Nancy, George!" she said warmly. "It's wonderful to see you." She set down the knife, walked over to the girls, and gave each of them a hug. She was a petite woman, considerably shorter than either of the girls. Nancy thought Mrs. Passano's chin-length brown hair, streaked blond by the sun, was extremely attractive.

"It's wonderful to be here," Nancy said.

"It sure is," George added.

Mrs. Passano smiled. "Why don't you two take showers and relax? We'll have time to catch up at dinner."

George and Nancy headed down a hallway toward the stairs. In the hallway, Nancy noticed that an old armchair was being used as a soft bed for a black-and-white cat. Paintings of horses and dogs hung on the walls, and a riding jacket lay tossed across a straight-backed chair. Nancy liked the house's cozy, lived-in look.

Upstairs, Nancy and George changed out of their jeans and took quick showers. Promptly at seven, they joined Laura and her mother at the dining-room table.

"Sit down, girls," Mrs. Passano said. "We're

having roast chicken and fresh vegetables that we grew ourselves." Mrs. Passano served the two girls the steaming food from a nearby platter.

"Mmm," Nancy said, inhaling the fragrant smell of the stuffing. "This reminds me of Hannah's special roast chicken dish." Hannah Gruen, the Drews' housekeeper, had lived with Nancy and her father, Carson Drew, ever since Nancy was three.

"Please give Hannah and your dad my best," Mrs. Passano told her. "I'm afraid Laura's dad is away on business. He's attending two auctions out of state. He's sorry he won't be able to see you."

"Mom has some exciting news," Laura said as she took a bite of her mashed potatoes. "A couple of months ago, she was named master of the hounds at the Mill River Hunt—the first woman ever."

Mrs. Passano smiled. "I was very lucky to get the job," she said modestly. "Unfortunately, the former master, Cameron Shaw, died last winter— in a fox-hunting accident. His horse fell while jumping a fence, and Cameron broke his neck. It was very sad. He and his wife were close friends of ours. It's been hard on her."

Nancy and George expressed sympathy, and everyone ate in silence for a minute. Nancy found herself brooding on the fact that the Passanos were into fox hunting. That was one sport she just didn't understand.

"I've ridden a lot, but I've never ridden in a fox hunt," Nancy admitted. "I don't think I'd have much fun chasing a fox."

"I totally agree," George chimed in. Nancy could hear a note of passion rising in her friend's voice.

"Oh, I feel the same way you do," Mrs. Passano said. Nancy looked at her in surprise. "Laura and I and many other riders at Mill River are against chasing foxes. In fact, one of my goals as master of the hounds is to persuade the Mill River board to make the hunt a drag hunt instead."

"A drag hunt?" Nancy asked, curious.

"That's when a fox's scent is dragged over the countryside for the hounds to follow. No live foxes are hunted," Laura explained, taking a bite of corn.

"That sounds much better," George declared.

"Unfortunately," Mrs. Passano said, "a few members of the board have been hard to convince. They're very traditional. They want the sport to remain the way it's always been. They think the real adventure is following the fox wherever it leads, rather than along a set path." She sighed. "It's going to be a real battle, because the vote has to be unanimous. I'll do everything I can to get them to change, though."

"I sure hope you succeed," George said. "But in the meantime—the poor fox!"

"Well, the fox is hardly ever caught," Laura

9

assured her. "In all my years of hunting, I've only seen one fox killed."

"Really?" Nancy asked, surprised and relieved.

"Sure. I mean, it's not like the hunt's aim is to hurt the fox," Laura said. "The point is to gallop around the countryside and have an exciting ride." Laura paused and studied her friends carefully. "Why don't you guys come out with us tomorrow and see for yourselves? You're both terrific riders."

Nancy hesitated. She still didn't like the idea of fox hunting. Catching George's worried glance, she could tell her friend felt the same way.

"Tomorrow's the last day of cubbing—the warm-up to the hunting season, when the huntsman works all the hounds," Mrs. Passano explained. "Opening day for the regular hunting season is in three days."

"How long does the regular hunting season last?" Nancy asked.

"The Mill River Hunt goes out every Saturday from the end of September to January," Mrs. Passano said. "After that it gets too cold to ride."

"You guys should really try it," Laura urged. "That way, you'll see what hunting's like firsthand. You might give us some fresh ideas on how to change the board's mind."

Nancy finished her potatoes while considering Laura's invitation. Maybe she *could* get some ideas on how to change the hunt. Glancing at George, she saw her shrug, then give a thumbs-up sign.

"Okay, we'll go, Laura," Nancy said.

Just then Nancy heard the front door open. Startled, she saw Peter Greenbriar burst into the dining room.

"Mrs. Passano," the groom announced breathlessly, "it's Dundee! She's on the floor of her stall, panting and wheezing. I'm scared she's not going to make it!"

2

A Bucketful of Trouble

Laura dropped her fork on her plate with a loud clatter. "Dundee?" she asked, her voice trembling. "But I just saw her before dinner. She was fine."

"I called the vet," Greenbriar said. "He'll be over right away. It's a good thing he lives nearby."

"Let's go, girls," Mrs. Passano said, quickly rising from her chair. She led the group out of the house and to the barn.

As they arrived, a Jeep screeched to a stop at the barn door. Nancy saw an older man climb out, carrying a black bag. He must be the vet, she thought. Without a word, he dashed into the barn.

Nancy could hear loud kicks on the sides of a stall down the aisle to the left as she followed Mrs. Passano.

"Let's stay outside," Mrs. Passano said. She stopped at a stall.

Peering over the half-door of the stall, Nancy watched as the dappled gray mare lay thrashing on the thick straw bedding. "It looks like she's struggling for breath," Nancy whispered to George.

Nancy watched anxiously as the vet pulled a syringe from his bag. After filling it with a liquid, he carefully injected it into the mare's neck. Then he capped the needle and put it in his jacket pocket.

Dundee calmed down, and the vet began to examine her. First, he listened to her heart with his stethoscope. Shaking his head, he moved up to Dundee's face and shone a small flashlight into her eyes and mouth.

Even from several feet away, Nancy could see flecks of foam around Dundee's lips.

"What could it be?" Mrs. Passano asked the vet as he continued to examine the horse. "I've never seen anything like this."

The vet didn't answer. Finally, Dundee's breathing gradually became more regular, and her thrashing legs fell still. The vet held up his finger, signaling that he'd answer in a moment. He took his stethoscope and listened again to the mare's heart.

"I think she'll be fine," he said softly—the first words he'd spoken that night.

"Thank goodness!" Laura exclaimed, her voice still shaky. "But what's wrong with her?"

"Well," the vet said slowly, taking off his tweed cap and fanning his face with it, "I can tell you, I don't think this horse has a disease. The symptoms would have shown up more gradually." He paused, choosing his words with care. "I'm going to take some blood to check for an infection or liver damage. But to be honest, I suspect she may have been poisoned."

Laura gasped. Her mother, who had entered the stall, looked at the vet, astonished. For a moment no one spoke.

"Mind you," the vet went on, "I won't be sure until I get the results of the blood work. And I'm not saying she was poisoned intentionally. She may have eaten something toxic by accident—something that made her very sick."

"But—but—" Nancy heard a man's voice stammering behind her. Turning around, she saw Peter Greenbriar hovering a few feet away. She'd completely forgotten he was there.

"This is—impossible," the groom said, wringing his hands. "I take good care of these horses. I watch them like my own children. I tell you, there's no way there could be an accidental poisoning in these stables."

"Peter," Mrs. Passano said, "no one thinks this is your fault. That hadn't even occurred to me. I know you're devoted to these horses. But I do want you to thoroughly inspect the stable. If Dundee *has* been poisoned, I want you to find what caused it before other horses are affected. The pasture will have to wait until it's light." Turning to the vet, she asked, "Do you have any idea what this poison could be?"

"Not really," he said. "There are a number of substances that could produce these symptoms. The blood test may tell us. I'd start by checking out the feed and water buckets, though."

"Mrs. Passano," Nancy said, leaning over the door of the stall as the vet drew blood from the horse, "now that Dundee's calm, would you mind if I came in and took a look around?"

"Not at all, Nancy, be my guest." Mrs. Passano looked up from where she sat stroking Dundee's head. "You're an experienced detective. You might really be able to help us. The more eyes on this job, the better. Laura and George, please take a look at the feed room. Peter, you can get started on the rest of the stable."

As everyone followed her directions, Nancy frowned. She didn't like too many people knowing she was a detective. Both the groom and the vet might have heard Mrs. Passano say she was.

Noticing the dim light in the stall, Nancy fetched a flashlight from the tack room, where she'd seen one earlier that day. Back at the stall, she unlatched the lower door and entered.

Mrs. Passano looked up. "Nancy, the feed and water buckets are over there, in the corners."

While the vet finished examining Dundee, Nancy headed to the bucket in the nearest corner and shone her flashlight inside.

There was an inch of clear water at the bottom of the bucket with a blade of hay floating in it. She knelt down and checked around the floor of the stall under the bucket. Where the straw lay thin in the corner, Nancy could see patches of the dirt floor showing through.

She moved over to the bucket in the other corner—the feed bucket, she reasoned—and pointed her flashlight inside. She saw only a few uneaten grains of feed, a mixture of oats and corn, and a yellow, powderlike substance. Ground corn? she wondered.

Once again, Nancy hunched down and shone the light on the ground under the empty bucket. In the straw, she spotted a few oats and pieces of corn that had fallen from the feed bucket. They, too, had yellow powder on them.

Was the powder part of Dundee's feed or something different? She ran a finger through the powder, then sniffed it. It had only a faint scent, but she didn't recognize it.

Nancy called over the vet and Mrs. Passano. "What's this yellow powder at the bottom of the feed bucket?" she asked. "Is this something that's normally added to a horse's feed?"

The vet stood and walked over to the bucket. He studied the powder under Nancy's flashlight beam. He ran a few grains of it between his thumb and forefinger, then sniffed it. "This is Taberol—a cattle feed," he announced. "It's poisonous to horses—not fatal, but it will make a horse very sick."

"Cattle feed?" Mrs. Passano repeated. "But we don't have any cattle feed in our barn."

"Could someone have bought some Taberol by mistake?" Nancy asked. "Thinking it was horse feed?"

"Not a chance," Mrs. Passano said. "Horse feed is a premixed grain made of oats and corn and a touch of molasses. No one could get it confused with a powder. And we add nothing to that feed. Peter can vouch for that."

"I don't know what to say," the vet said, scratching his head. "If there's no Taberol in the barn, how could it have gotten into the feed? Unless someone brought it in on purpose, intending to mix it into the feed. But why?"

That's exactly what I'd like to find out, Nancy thought. "If someone wanted to poison a horse," she said, turning to the vet, "would tampering with its feed be a good plan? It seems like it would be pretty risky. What if the horse didn't feel like eating all its dinner?"

"Most horses have huge appetites," Mrs. Passano pointed out. "That's one thing we can depend on. Dundee never misses a meal."

"In that case," Nancy said slowly, "why didn't it work? Either the culprit didn't know the exact amount of Taberol needed for a fatal dose, or else he meant to make Dundee sick but not to kill her."

"You're absolutely right," the vet agreed. "I couldn't have put it better myself." He reached into his bag. "Since we now know what caused Dundee's reaction, I can give her an injection to counteract the effects. She should be back to normal in twenty-four hours."

Just then Nancy heard a rustling noise a few feet away. Turning, she saw Peter Greenbriar hovering in the shadows of the stall. His gaze flicked over the group gathered around the feed bucket. Surprised, Nancy took a step back—she hadn't even heard him come into the stall. Had he been trying to eavesdrop?

As if reading her thoughts, the groom quickly said to Mrs. Passano, "Just wanted you to know I checked out the other stalls and the tack room. There's nothing out of place there, ma'am."

"Thanks, Peter," Mrs. Passano said. "Ah, here come Laura and George," she added as the two girls walked up to the stall door. "Find anything?"

"Nothing," Laura replied, sounding discouraged. George shook her head.

Nancy stepped around Dundee, who was resting peacefully, and walked over to Peter Greenbriar. "Would you show me around the rest of the stable?" she asked, hoping for a chance to question him in more detail. Since he was the groom, she reasoned, he would have been around the stable most of the day. If pressed, he might remember something important. "I'd like to get an idea of how someone could have come in here without being noticed."

"It would be hard for anyone to get by me," he insisted. "I watch this place like a hawk."

"Well, someone must have sneaked by you to put the Taberol in Dundee's feed," Nancy pointed out.

Greenbriar looked down at his shoes and said nothing.

"Why don't we start with the office?" Nancy suggested, heading into the aisle between the stalls. "I noticed one next to the tack room earlier today. Is it *your* office?"

"Yes," the groom said, following her away from Dundee's stall. "I use it to order supplies and to schedule appointments—like if someone wants to come over and look at a horse. I also keep files on the horses' pedigrees and health. Mr. Passano does the business accounts from his office in the house."

"I see," Nancy said. As she followed him into

the office, she asked, "Did you notice anything out of the ordinary at the barn today, or within the past few days?"

"Not a thing," he answered.

Suddenly, they heard a loud gasp. "Hey, everybody!" Laura called out. "Come here, quick!"

Nancy dashed out of the office and looked around for Laura.

"Over here," Laura said, gesturing frantically from Morning Glory's stall, right next to Dundee's.

Nancy ran over. "Laura, what is it?" she asked.

Nancy's friend looked distraught. "I just checked the names on the horses' feed buckets," she said. "Morning Glory's and Dundee's buckets were switched!" Laura paused, her lower lip trembling. "It wasn't Dundee they were trying to poison. It was Morning Glory!"

3

Tallyho

"Switched?" Peter Greenbriar repeated, coming up behind Nancy. "That's impossible!"

"What is it, Laura?" Mrs. Passano asked as she strolled over from the barn door, where she'd just said good night to the vet.

"Morning Glory got Dundee's bucket," Laura said breathlessly, "and vice versa. You can see Dundee's name, right here." Nancy looked at the piece of white tape wrapped around the feed bucket's handle. Sure enough, there was *Dundee*, written in tiny black letters along the lower edge.

"And Morning Glory's bucket is in Dundee's stall," George added, peering around from the stall next door.

Mrs. Passano turned to the groom. "Please tell me exactly what happened during feeding time,

Peter," she said sternly. "How could these buckets have been switched?"

The groom licked his lips nervously, then said, "Right before I fed the horses tonight, I took the buckets to the feed room to wash them. Then I put feed in them. I guess someone could have sneaked into the feed room and slipped in the poison while I was taking buckets to horses at the far end of the barn."

Mrs. Passano stared at him, her green eyes narrowing. "And?" she asked sternly. "What then?"

"Well," he muttered, "I suppose I—I could have mixed up the two buckets." He took a deep breath, then added, "By accident, of course."

Mrs. Passano looked annoyed. "Well, I think it's time to call it a night, everyone," she said. "Peter, you'll have to check on Dundee several times during the night. If there's any change, call me immediately." She turned to Nancy and George. "Peter lives in the apartment above the barn," she explained.

The groom nodded his head. "I'll do anything I can to help. Well, then, good night." Giving a quick wave, he walked toward the barn door and disappeared into the night.

As she left the barn with the others, Nancy noticed a white staircase going up the outer wall of the barn to a door just below roof level—Peter Greenbriar's apartment, she guessed.

Back at the house, Mrs. Passano offered chocolate cake and milk to the three girls. Sitting around the kitchen table, they ate in silence. Nancy leaned back in her chair and closed her eyes, feeling exhausted. It had been a long day, and if she was going cubbing tomorrow, she knew she ought to go to bed.

But she couldn't help thinking about the events of the evening. Was Peter Greenbriar telling the truth? And which horse was the real target? But the question that nagged her most of all was, why would someone *want* to poison one of the horses?

"Nancy," Laura said, breaking into her thoughts, "I know I invited you and George here for a few days of riding . . ." Laura paused, and Nancy guessed what was coming next. "But I know that you've solved a lot of cases around River Heights, and . . ." She glanced away shyly.

"I'd love to take on this case," Nancy said at once. "As your houseguest, I'll be able to investigate undercover." Though Peter Greenbriar may already know I'm a detective, she thought.

"That's wonderful, Nancy," Mrs. Passano said, smiling. "We sure could use your help. I'm worried sick about the horses."

"Has anything else happened around the farm recently?" Nancy asked. "Anything unusual?"

"Nothing strange has happened around the farm," Mrs. Passano answered slowly. "There *was* an odd incident during a cub hunt last week,

23

though. A huge tree was lying across a path, and when the horses jerked to a sudden stop, one rider fell off and broke his leg. Well, it turned out that the tree had been cut down on purpose—we noticed it had saw and ax marks on the trunk."

"Did the person who owned the land know anything about it?" Nancy asked.

"Nothing," Mrs. Passano confirmed. "You see, the hunt club has permission from all the local landowners to hunt over their farms, but the club maintains all the actual riding trails. Normally, we would've been told by the landowner beforehand if a tree had fallen onto the trail. That way, we could clear it away. After the rider fell, as master of the hounds, I called the landowner. He knew nothing about the tree."

"Do you really think these two incidents are connected?" George asked. "A tree in the woods on another farm, and a horse being poisoned here?"

"Well, it's something to keep in mind," Nancy said. She paused, then asked, "What about Peter Greenbriar? He had the opportunity to add the Taberol. He seemed kind of defensive."

Laura and her mother exchanged glances. "I'll grant you," Mrs. Passano said, "he was acting a bit strangely tonight. I think he was worried about being blamed. And he should be. Giving a horse the wrong feed is grounds for being fired. But I'll vouch for his character. He manages the horses wonderfully. He may have had the opportunity—but certainly no motive."

That remains to be seen, Nancy thought. "How long has he worked for you?" she asked.

"For just about a year," Laura said. "Before us, he worked for Charles Jackson, a neighboring horse breeder, for many years."

"Girls," Mrs. Passano said, rising from her chair, "I know you're worried and would like to solve this problem tonight. But if we're going cubbing tomorrow, we all need a good night's sleep. The hunt starts at six-thirty sharp."

"Why so early?" George asked.

"This time of year, it gets too hot by midday. Everyone feels sluggish," Laura answered.

"Like the way I'm feeling now," Nancy said, covering up a yawn as she got up to set her dishes by the sink.

As Nancy followed Mrs. Passano, Laura, and George upstairs, she thought of the horses. She hoped they would sleep safely that night.

"George, you look great!" Nancy exclaimed the next morning, admiring her friend's tall, trim figure in Mrs. Passano's breeches and black hunt coat. Nancy had borrowed a similar outfit from Laura. "You look like you belong on a horse."

"Well, let's just hope I can stay on," George said with a wry smile, picking up the helmet she had also borrowed.

"Don't kid yourself. You're a terrific rider." Nancy clapped George on the back, and the two girls hurried downstairs to grab glasses of juice and some slices of toast before joining the Passanos at the barn.

Outside the stable, Mrs. Passano was hitching a horse trailer up to her pickup truck. "Here, girls," she said, handing Nancy and George lead ropes. "You bring out your horses while I get my hunter, Trimble. And by the way, Dundee is fine. She's on her feet, eating her morning hay."

Just then Laura appeared, proudly leading Morning Glory out the barn door. Even in the dim light of dawn, the horse gleamed, his coal-black coat shimmering.

Nancy caught her breath. "Laura, I have never seen such a beautiful horse," she said.

Laura smiled and patted Morning Glory on his neck. After guiding him into the trailer, she helped Nancy and George load their horses. Once all the horses were secured in the trailer, the girls joined Mrs. Passano in the pickup.

As they drove to the hunt's meeting place, at a farm four miles away, Nancy felt curious about how the day would go. She loved the idea of riding on trails through beautiful countryside. But she hated the idea of chasing a fox. She hoped Laura was right—that they probably wouldn't catch the fox.

Mrs. Passano pulled the pickup next to another trailer in a grassy field, and everyone climbed out. They unloaded the horses, and then saddled and bridled them. The sun was now up, and the day promised to be gorgeous—warm with a hint of crispness in the air. Under a turquoise-colored sky, the field hummed with activity.

Nancy and George were fascinated at the turn-out of people—crusty old sportsmen on sleek hunters alongside children on shaggy ponies. Surrounding a large, red-haired man on horseback were at least forty fox hounds—white-, brown-, and black-spotted dogs with smooth coats and big brown eyes.

Gazing around, Nancy took in the surrounding countryside with its gently rolling hills. Lush green meadows were broken up by small groves of trees, their leaves just starting to turn color, and larger patches of woods beyond.

George sighed. "Frankly, Nan, I'm having second thoughts about coming out here today. Hunting a fox just isn't my idea of fun."

"I'm feeling the same way," Nancy admitted.

Just then she noticed the red-haired man on horseback calling in a high-pitched yelp to the hounds. As the hounds began to mill excitedly around him, Nancy asked Laura who he was.

"That's Grant Hathaway," Laura told her. "He's the huntsman, which is the next official in rank after the master of the hounds. He directs the hounds and makes sure they pick up the fox's scent."

"How does he make the hounds obey?" George asked.

"He controls them through calls and also by sounding his horn," Laura explained. "He also takes care of the hounds. He transports them to each hunt meet. He has two assistants, called the whippers-in. There they are now." She pointed to two other men rounding up the hounds. "Samuel and Duncan Burnet. That's the whole hunt board: the Burnet brothers, my mom, Mr. Hathaway, and one local landowner."

"So what exactly does your mom do as master of the hounds?" Nancy asked.

"She's in charge of leading all the horses and riders," Laura told her. "She makes sure that the riders follow the huntsman without getting too close or interfering with the hounds."

"How can you be sure that there's always a fox to chase?" George asked.

"That's the easy part," Laura said. "Foxes live all over this countryside in covers—groves of trees or thick hedges. It's the huntsman's job to know where these covers are. But if anyone spots a fox before the huntsman does, they call out 'Tallyho' to let him know." Laura mounted Morning Glory, who was prancing about in excitement. Nancy and George mounted their horses, too.

"Hello, Laura," Grant Hathaway, the huntsman, called over to her. "Where's your mother? I have to warn her—Mark Plonsky's here again."

"Over there," Laura replied, pointing to her mother on the far side of the pickup. "I'm sure she'll be interested in *that* news."

"Who's Mark Plonsky?" Nancy asked when the huntsman had turned in Mrs. Passano's direction.

"He leads some local protesters who are totally opposed to fox hunting." Laura pointed out a group of about eight people on foot, who were hanging around the edge of the field.

Nancy picked out their leader, a handsome, dark-haired young guy, who was gesturing wildly to his companions and pointing to the hounds. "What's wrong with that?" she asked.

"Well, they come to the hunts and really stir up trouble," Laura said. "It's too bad. Plenty of Mill River riders sympathize with Mark's commitment to animal rights, but they get turned off by his pushiness. That makes it even harder for my mom to persuade the board to change to a drag hunt. And besides, he's trespassing, but the police don't have the manpower to chase the trespassers away during every hunt."

"What do you mean about his being pushy?" George asked.

"He's never even tried to meet with the hunt board to discuss his point of view," Laura said. "He just showed up at the hunt one day and

29

sabotaged it by imitating Mr. Hathaway's call. He totally confused the hounds. They started following Mark and his buddies instead of the fox's scent. He could approach us in a civilized way, but he thinks we're all horrible fox killers. He won't even talk to us. In fact, I'm not even sure that he knows my mother's trying to change the hunt to a drag hunt."

Nancy suspected that if Mark Plonsky *did* know, it might not change things. He might feel he had to keep the pressure on until the entire board agreed. But she knew this wasn't the place to argue with Laura. "I bet he drives Mr. Hathaway crazy," she said.

"That's for sure!" Laura said, rolling her eyes. "Mr. Hathaway is an old friend of our family's, but he's totally opposed to changing Mill River to a drag hunt. Mark really drives him nuts."

Just then Mr. Hathaway sounded the horn, to signal the beginning of the hunt. As the hounds leaped forward, Nancy felt Hopscotch quiver with anticipation.

Mrs. Passano led the hunt field off at a short distance behind the huntsmen and whippers-in. They trotted, then broke into a canter as they approached a stream beside a grove of trees. The horses splashed across the stream and headed for the trees, as the hounds disappeared down a path ahead.

Quickly, the hounds led the riders through the

trees, then paused at the edge of a meadow, sniffing frantically.

"George, look!" Nancy exclaimed softly, pulling up beside her friend. She pointed to a red fox running over the crest of a distant hill.

"Run, fox, run," George murmured. "Get away!"

"Tallyho!" a voice called out. The hounds raced forward, barking loudly as the fox disappeared over the hill. Mrs. Passano galloped through the meadow, straight toward a rail fence.

Nancy hunched down over Hopscotch's neck as she, too, galloped across the meadow. Laura streaked past. Morning Glory raised his head, anticipating the jump about twenty yards away.

Suddenly, Mr. Hathaway, Mrs. Passano, and the riders close behind them veered to the side.

"Stop!" Mrs. Passano shouted. "Don't jump! Barbed wire!"

Across the top of the fence ahead, someone had strung barbed wire. Its sharp points glinted menacingly in the bright autumn sunshine.

Nancy instantly pulled on the reins and sat deep in the saddle. Any horse that jumped over the barbed wire was sure to be seriously injured!

4

A Well-Dressed Fox

The horse ahead of Nancy kicked and slid. Hopscotch reared back, and Nancy was nearly thrown. She clutched wildly at Hopscotch's mane, hanging on desperately. Using all her strength, she regained her balance as the mare's front hooves thumped down.

Pulling the mare sharply to the right, Nancy steered her to a safe place alongside the fence.

As she soothed the skittish mare, Nancy studied the fence. The thin wire with its pointed barbs had been wound around the top of the fence posts and run along the top of the rail. Why would someone do such a thing?

Suddenly, she heard Laura gasp behind her. Turning around, Nancy saw George pulling on Lancelot's right reins, trying to steer him away from the fence. As Lancelot wheeled to the right,

George lost her balance and fell off. Luckily, she landed a few feet away from his hooves.

The horse thundered off across the field. George stood up and brushed herself off.

"Are you okay, George?" Nancy asked, riding over.

"I'll live," George said dryly. "Unless I die of embarrassment first."

"Don't be silly," Laura said. "Every good rider takes a tumble now and then. Otherwise, you're not challenging yourself."

George laughed. "Well, the next challenge will be finding Lancelot. Did you see where he went?"

"Mr. Zachary, that man over there, caught him," Laura said. She pointed to a disgruntled-looking older man on a gray horse who was slowly heading toward them, holding on to Lancelot's reins.

Nancy and Laura watched as George retrieved Lancelot from Mr. Zachary. As George tried to mount the horse again, Lancelot danced away from her, tossing his head and snorting. Mr. Zachary dismounted, gave his reins to another rider nearby, and helped George settle the horse. Then he gave George a leg up before he remounted.

After chatting with Mr. Zachary for a moment, George returned to Nancy and Laura. "Whew!" George said, shaking her head. "That guy sure has it in for the animal activists. He's saying they sabotaged this jump. He also said he's sure the chopped-down tree in the woods last week was Plonsky's work."

"He could be right," Laura declared.

"He said it was part of their plan to put an end to Mill River," George went on. " 'They're stepping up their tactics,' he said. Boy, was he mad!" George looked back at the man, who was talking excitedly to Mrs. Passano.

"Well," Nancy said, "if the animal activists are behind this sabotage, then they've gone too far. The horses could really have been hurt on the barbed wire."

"I'm all for helping the fox," Laura said, "but I don't want the horses injured."

Nancy nodded, thinking. Were the animal activists guilty? Would they let other animals get hurt, just to achieve their ends?

And what if the hunt sabotage was related to the poisoning at Sky Meadow Farm the night before? Had the poisoner deliberately given a dose large enough to make the horse sick but not large enough to kill her? Would someone who loved animals have masterminded that?

Glancing over, she noticed that Laura and George had ridden toward Mrs. Passano, who was gathering the horses and riders together again. Nancy scanned the crowd for Mark Plonsky and his fellow activists, but she saw only horses and riders. No one was on foot. On the far edges of the field, there were only trees and horizon.

"Excuse me," Nancy said to a girl her age who was sitting on a horse nearby. "Do the animal activists usually follow the hunt everywhere?"

"They try to," the girl replied, biting her lip and glancing around anxiously. "But since they travel on foot, they can't always keep up."

Nancy nodded. Noticing the girl's distracted manner, she asked, "Are you okay?"

"Oh, I'm just looking for my friend Alexa Shaw," the girl said. "She's supposed to be here today, but I haven't seen her. I spoke to her just last night, and she was planning to come."

Nancy frowned. Alexa Shaw . . . The name sounded familiar, but she couldn't place it.

Then, suddenly, she remembered. Wasn't that the daughter of Mrs. Passano's friend, whose father had been master of the hunt? She was the girl Laura said had wanted to buy Morning Glory so badly.

"Maybe she woke up sick this morning," Nancy said.

"Maybe," the girl said doubtfully.

Nancy watched as Mrs. Passano, Mr. Zachary, and another man carefully stripped the barbed wire from the fence. Even though they were wearing gloves, they had to work very slowly. Finally, they wound the wire into a coil and put it to the side of the fence. Then Mrs. Passano announced to the crowd that the fence was safe to jump.

After blowing his huntsman's horn, Grant Hathaway jumped the fence and directed the hounds into the next field. After waiting a minute to give the huntsman a lead, Mrs. Passano followed, with the riders close behind. Nancy took the jump easily on Hopscotch, then charged up the hill. To her immediate right was Laura. Nancy admired her friend's graceful form as Morning Glory galloped effortlessly up the hill.

George, to Nancy's left, gave Nancy a gleeful smile as she urged Lancelot onward.

"What is this—a race?" Nancy yelled, grinning at George. Letting out a whoop, George galloped past Nancy.

The riders jumped several more fences, including a wooden triangular structure called a chicken coop. Nancy looked at the riders ahead of her. They had slowed down and were entering a wooded area. There was a narrow path down a hill. The horses followed one another single file. They crossed a stream at the bottom. Then everyone paused, listening for the hounds.

"What a fabulous run," Nancy heard someone murmur behind her. "I'll bet Charles Jackson's new hunt won't be as good as this."

Turning, Nancy saw the girl who'd been looking for Alexa Shaw. She was talking to Mr. Zachary, the older man who'd helped George with Lancelot.

"Charles will be lucky if he can even get decent

runs," Mr. Zachary scoffed in a low voice. "His hounds aren't trained yet, and his hunt isn't recognized by any official fox-hunting association. He'll never be able to attract riders away from us. If you ask me, he was nuts to leave Mill River."

"Quiet!" another rider said. "I'm trying to hear the hounds."

The horses moved forward again, trotting deeper into the woods. Guiding Hopscotch, Nancy wondered about the conversation she'd just overheard. Charles Jackson was Peter Greenbriar's former employer, she remembered. Why would he have wanted to leave the Mill River Hunt? And why had he started up his own hunt? Nancy wanted to learn more.

At that moment the horses in front began to pick up speed. The sun shone through the trees, dappling the woodland with light. Birds chirped on either side, and patches of asters and goldenrod brightened the forest glades. Nancy realized that the day had grown quite warm. She wanted to unbutton her hunt coat, but the horses were beginning to canter. She needed to keep both hands on the reins.

The hounds started to bay loudly. Nancy guessed that they'd picked up the fox's scent. As the horses galloped down the trail, Nancy had to concentrate on controlling Hopscotch, not allowing her to get too close to Morning Glory, who was just ahead.

The path took a sharp turn to the right. As she rode around the corner, Nancy saw the trail open up into a small clearing.

Suddenly, the horses before her came to a crashing halt. It was just like a pileup of cars on a highway. Horses reared up and shied, and riders collided with one another.

What's going on? Nancy wondered, scouting around for the cause of the trouble.

Finally, she got a clear view into the glade. Nancy couldn't believe her eyes!

In the middle of the clearing was a big stuffed fox—at least as tall as she was—standing upright and dressed in formal hunting clothes, complete with top hat, boots, and red coat!

Hopscotch remained calm at the sight, but Nancy saw Morning Glory, terrified, backing into a nearby tree. Laura was trying desperately to control him.

Nancy gasped as she saw Laura's helmet hit a low-hanging branch—with a hornet's nest hanging from it!

A swarm of hornets buzzed out, circling around angrily. Nancy winced. In seconds, the enraged hornets would strike their target—Morning Glory and Laura.

5

Angry Protests

Quickly, Nancy rode over to Morning Glory. While controlling her own horse, Nancy reached out and caught the reins on Morning Glory's bridle and yanked him away from the nest. Morning Glory gave a small buck. Laura, surprised and thrown off balance, clung tightly onto his mane. Nancy realized Morning Glory had been stung!

Holding her breath, she watched the angry cloud of hornets swarm overhead, then buzz back into the nest. She sighed in relief.

"Easy, boy, easy," Laura murmured, stroking her horse's neck. "Calm down. Everything's all right." Looking up at Nancy, she said, "Thanks, Nan. You're a better rider than you give yourself credit for. Not many riders could have pulled off a maneuver like that. You saved Morning Glory and me from being badly stung. I didn't even see those hornets till it was too late."

"I'm glad I saw them in time," Nancy said. "Those stings really hurt. And a whole swarm of them . . . I hope Morning Glory's okay."

"He'll be fine," Laura assured her.

Morning Glory's flank was quivering where he'd been stung, but otherwise, Nancy noticed, he was calm. She was amazed at how steady he was.

"Why don't the police just haul Plonsky away?" Nancy heard a young man say. "He's endangering people's lives, and he's trespassing!" Many riders nodded, and a couple of loud shouts of agreement rang through the hunt crowd.

Nancy dismounted and handed Hopscotch's reins to Laura. Then she walked up to the stuffed fox in the clearing and leaned over to examine it. It was human-size, stuffed with straw, and stuck on a pole. Nancy could see why the riders would blame the animal activists for putting it there. The fox's hunting outfit was an obvious reference to their cause.

As Nancy inspected the fox's clothes, she noticed that all the tags had been cut out. No clues there, she thought. She searched around on the ground but found nothing except a few bits of straw.

Then, out of the corner of her eye, Nancy noticed something brown a short distance away. A dead leaf? she wondered. Walking over and bending down, she saw a brown leather glove.

Nancy picked it up and looked it over. It had a Velcro closure at the wrist. Inside was a tag: Marburg's Saddlery Shop. No size was printed on the tag. Nancy judged that the glove could fit either a man or a woman, though not a large man.

Nancy searched around for the other glove but didn't find it. This glove was probably dropped by the person who had set up the stuffed fox, Nancy guessed. Slipping the glove into her pocket, she felt excited. Finally—a clue!

Nancy quickly returned to Hopscotch. After taking the reins from Laura, she remounted the horse.

"Ladies and gentlemen," Mrs. Passano said to the riders as Grant Hathaway and the Burnet brothers called the straggling hounds together. Nancy noticed that many of the riders looked anxious, but a few were scowling and muttering angrily.

"I'm glad to see no one's been hurt," Mrs. Passano said. "Thanks to your quick reactions, we've avoided any serious accidents today. You're all probably very upset. But I promise to get to the bottom of these awful tricks. I *will* find out who is sabotaging the Mill River Hunt and why. And that person will definitely be punished."

A general murmur of support spread through the group. "Hear, hear," Mr. Zachary shouted.

"I'm going on to finish today's hunt," Mrs. Passano added. "We'll ride at a slower pace to minimize the danger. I hope you will all join me."

"Someone wants to discourage us from hunting," a thin man in his thirties added gravely. "But we can't let them push us around. We must not give in to sabotage!"

To Nancy's surprise, most of the riders, including Mr. Zachary, turned around to ride home. Some were muttering that they'd had enough hunting mishaps for one day. Only a few others, including Laura, rode off behind Mrs. Passano.

George rode over to Nancy. "What're you going to do, Nan?" she asked. "Give in to sabotage?"

Nancy laughed. "Well, I wouldn't put it that way, George, but since you mention it, I do think I'll call it a day." Stifling a yawn, she added, "It's been a long time since I've ridden. I'm exhausted."

"Me, too," George said. "Plus, this whole hunting thing just bugs me too much."

"I was glad to see how easily the fox outsmarted the hounds," Nancy commented as they guided their horses back up the trail.

"True," George agreed. "I guess foxes really *are* sly. Still, I'd like to see Mrs. Passano win the hunt board over and make this a drag hunt."

"I couldn't agree more," Nancy said.

On their way back, Nancy told George about

the glove. Then she fell silent, thinking about the strange sabotage incidents.

At the Passanos' horse trailer, the two girls dismounted and untacked their horses. They rubbed them down with towels, put sweat sheets on them, then walked them until they cooled down. Then they led them back into the trailer.

A few feet away, Nancy spotted Mark Plonsky arguing with Mr. Zachary. The older man looked furious. He was waving his arms and scowling fiercely. Finally, Mr. Zachary smacked one fist into his other palm and stomped away.

Nancy was surprised to see that Mark Plonsky seemed unfazed. He merely raised an eyebrow as he watched Mr. Zachary walk away.

"George," Nancy said, "I'll be right back."

Strolling over to Mark Plonsky, Nancy noticed that he was only a couple of years older than she was. Medium-tall with wavy dark hair and light gray eyes, he wore blue jeans and a green flannel shirt with the sleeves rolled up. Nancy wondered whether the glove she'd found might fit him, but he had his hands in his jeans pockets.

"Hello," Nancy said, smiling at Mark Plonsky. "I'm Nancy Drew, a guest of Laura Passano's."

"Yes?" he said impatiently. "What can I do for you? I can't talk long. My friends are waiting." He glanced over at the other protesters, who were clustered around a burgundy-colored minivan about thirty feet away.

"Well," Nancy said slowly, trying to figure out how to loosen up the guy, "Mr. Zachary seemed so mad. I wanted to make sure that everything's okay."

A wry smile lit up the activist's face. "Thank you for thinking of me, but I can take care of myself."

"What was he so angry about, anyway?" Nancy asked.

"It's really not any of your business," Plonsky said. "But if you must know, he blames me for the sabotage today." He rolled his eyes, as if the idea was ridiculous.

"Well . . . I've heard you sabotaged the hunt before," Nancy said. "You weren't responsible for the barbed wire and the stuffed fox?"

He shook his head. "Unlike you fox hunters," he declared, "I'd never put an animal in danger— fox, hound, or horse." Then he abruptly turned and went to join the other activists. Nancy watched them pile into the minivan and drive away.

Nancy went back to the horse trailer and told George about her conversation. "Mark Plonsky has a real attitude problem," Nancy said. "It's hard to tell if he's lying or not."

"He probably assumes you're just another hunter who doesn't care about the fox," George said thoughtfully. "That could be why he was so rude."

"Maybe," Nancy said. "But I still can't rule him out as a suspect. Except . . ." She leaned against the horse trailer. "I can't imagine him poisoning Dundee. And I have this gut feeling that the two events are connected somehow. I still don't know how or why—but I'm determined to find out."

Back at Sky Meadow Farm, Nancy took a shower and changed into a blue cotton skirt, sandals, and a blue-and-white-striped T-shirt. Downstairs, she and George helped Mrs. Passano set the patio table for a late lunch, while Laura made tuna salad. Nancy had decided to wait until after lunch to show the Passanos the glove. She needed their undivided attention. There had been no time on the ride back, and guests were coming for lunch.

"It's like a summer day," Mrs. Passano said, shading her eyes as she looked out over the hills beyond the patio. "It was really too warm for hunting, but at least we didn't hit any more traps."

"When are the Shaws arriving?" Laura asked.

"Here they are now," Mrs. Passano said, waving cheerfully as Mrs. Shaw and her daughter, Alexa, pulled up the driveway in their car.

Nancy looked up with interest as the Shaws parked, got out of their car, and crossed the side yard to the patio. Maybe she'd find out why Alexa hadn't met her friend at the cubbing meet earlier.

Laura introduced Nancy and George to the Shaws. Mrs. Shaw was a plump, middle-aged woman with short gray hair and a fluttery manner. Alexa was very pretty—tall and slim, with long flaxen blond hair—but Nancy could see why Laura didn't like her. Alexa shook hands with Nancy and George and then moved away, her mouth fixed in a pout. Her large gold earrings and shimmery silk dress seemed to Nancy a bit much for a casual lunch with friends.

"How was the hunt today?" Mrs. Shaw asked.

"Awful," Mrs. Passano answered. She told the Shaws about the sabotage as she served everyone tuna salad, tomato slices, and crusty French bread.

"I'm glad I wasn't there," Alexa declared. "My horse went lame at the last minute. With my luck, I'll have to miss Opening Day."

"Your horse went lame?" Mrs. Passano asked, concerned. "I'm so sorry."

"I do wish Alexa would give up hunting," Mrs. Shaw said fretfully. "It's so dangerous." Mrs. Shaw eyed her daughter nervously. Alexa glanced away, looking annoyed. Recalling that Mrs. Shaw's husband had died riding in a hunt the year before, Nancy felt sorry for the widow. No wonder she was feeling protective of her daughter.

"I can take care of myself, Mom," Alexa put in.

"I know that, darling," Mrs. Shaw replied. "Still, I can't help worrying." She took a bite of tuna salad, then turned to Nancy and George. "And how did you girls like hunting?"

"It was fun to gallop over the countryside,"

Nancy said. "But I don't think I'll hunt again. Unless they make it a drag hunt, that is."

"I totally agree," George said. "I couldn't face chasing another poor fox."

"You and the animal activists," Alexa said sourly. "I guess they're the ones behind these pranks."

"That's what most of the riders think," Mrs. Passano admitted.

"And what about you, Maggie?" Mrs. Shaw asked, looking at her friend.

"Well, I suspect they're responsible," Mrs. Passano said. "Even though I sympathize with Mark's cause, I certainly don't approve of his tactics. What if a rider got hurt? I believe in changing the system from within, not terrorizing from outside." Mrs. Passano spoke passionately, her green eyes gleaming in the afternoon sun.

Nancy realized that Laura's mother must be torn between her love of animals and her devotion to the Mill River Hunt. She hoped Mrs. Passano could change the board's mind about adopting a drag hunt. And even more than that, she hoped that the saboteur—and the poisoner—would be caught soon.

After lunch the Shaws went home, and Mrs. Passano and Laura went upstairs for a nap. Anxious to tackle the case, Nancy suggested to George that they check the barn for more clues to Dundee's poisoning.

When they reached the stable, the girls saw that most of the stalls were full. The horses were either resting after the hunt or just staying out of the warm afternoon sun. Except for the drowsy sounds of swishing tails and soft snorts, the barn was quiet. Peter Greenbriar was nowhere to be seen.

"It's so peaceful here," George said. "It's hard to believe that someone who tried to poison a horse was lurking around last evening."

Nancy raised her eyebrows. "Let's just hope it stays peaceful."

George offered to check out the stalls again, while Nancy went to search the feed room and tack room. She knew that Laura and George had checked them out the night before, but she wanted to take a fresh look in the light of day.

In the feed room, Nancy lifted the lid of a wooden bin and saw a grain mixture inside. The horse feed smelled sweet, she thought, like molasses. She reached into the bin and sifted some feed through her hand. It felt granular and slightly sticky. Finding nothing unusual, Nancy went next door to the tack room.

She scanned the tack room, noticing several neat racks of saddles and bridles, each labeled with a horse's name. The wooden bins in this room held a jumble of helmets, paddock boots, spurs, and brushes. After several minutes of fruitless searching, Nancy went out to find George.

"I couldn't find a thing, Nancy," George said.

"There's one more place I want to search," Nancy told her. "Peter Greenbriar's office. Could you be my lookout, in case he shows up?"

"I'd love to," George said, grinning. "There's something about that man I just don't trust."

Nancy slipped into the office. Quickly, she leafed through the files on Dundee and Morning Glory but found nothing of interest. The only things in the side drawers of Greenbriar's desk were yellow notepads and a phone book for nearby Baltimore. The top drawer held a calendar and a few pens and pencils. Poring over the calendar, Nancy saw some appointments with vets and feed shippers, but nothing significant.

She groped around one more time in the back of the top drawer. Her hand touched something—stiff paper.

Quickly, she pulled it out. It was a snapshot of Morning Glory, standing unsaddled in a paddock.

Turning it over, she noticed a spot of clear glue, with a few grains of yellow powder in it.

Nancy started. That powder—it looked just like Taberol!

6

A Poisonous Picture

Nancy slid the snapshot of Morning Glory into her pocket. It had to be an important lead. She ran out of the office to tell George.

In a hushed voice, Nancy told George what she'd found. Aware that Peter Greenbriar might be close by, the two girls hurried back to the house to discuss the new clue in private.

Upstairs in their room, Nancy showed George the snapshot. George switched on a bedside lamp and studied the photo in the pool of light. "Weird," she said, turning the photo over to see the spot of powder on the back. "What do you make of this, Nan?"

Nancy thought for a moment. "I think this means that Morning Glory definitely *was* the target," she mused. "Maybe this photo just fell off something in the Sky Meadow files and got lost in

Peter Greenbriar's drawer. But if the Passanos don't recognize the picture, I'll bet it was left by the poisoner. The yellow powder on it is just too suspicious."

"You're telling me," George agreed. "It looks like someone really has it in for Morning Glory."

Nancy sighed, her blue eyes troubled. "I can't believe someone would target a horse this way," she said indignantly. "But why was the picture in Peter Greenbriar's drawer? And how did it get Taberol on it?"

"He might have been keeping the stuff in his desk drawer," George said.

"But I didn't see any other traces of it there," Nancy said. She frowned, trying to make sense of it all. "Suppose the person who wanted to poison Morning Glory hired a stranger to do the dirty work," she thought out loud. "This photo could have been given to the stranger to help him or her identify the right horse."

"Well, that theory lets Peter Greenbriar off the hook," George pointed out. "He already knows Morning Glory."

"I'm not letting him off the hook just yet," Nancy declared. "But here's another scenario. What if the culprit dropped the photo in the drawer accidentally while searching for something—like a file?"

"A file?" George asked, looking puzzled. "What kind of file?"

"If the sabotage at the hunt and the horse poisoning *are* connected," Nancy reasoned, "the poisoner could have been searching for information on the Mill River Hunt. The Passanos' barn would be a logical place to look, since Mrs. Passano is master of the hounds. And if he or she was in the barn anyway—"

"You're not saying the animal activists are behind this," George protested. "They love animals. They wouldn't poison a horse."

"But remember, there wasn't enough Taberol to kill a horse," Nancy reminded her friend. "It may have been meant only as a scare. Mark Plonsky could be trying to put pressure on the hunt club by attacking the Passanos' farm. He could have gotten this photo somewhere and given it to one of the other activists to identify Morning Glory."

George frowned. "I don't know, Nan." She paused. "What about one of the bidders for Morning Glory, like Alexa Shaw?" she suggested. "Someone might have been really bitter about Laura's outbidding them at the auction. They might want to get back at her by poisoning him."

"Maybe," Nancy replied. She fell silent, considering that possibility.

"What do you make of the glue spot?" George went on, breaking into Nancy's thoughts.

Nancy picked up the photo and touched the spot gently, careful not to dislodge the specks of powder. "It still feels a little sticky, like it came from a glue stick," she commented, handing it over to George. "Maybe the poisoner ripped the picture from a photo album?" Nancy sat down, her mind spinning. At this point in her investigation, there were too many questions and not enough answers.

"Why don't we see if Laura and her mother are awake," George suggested. "I'm sure they'll want to know about this new twist as soon as possible."

"Good idea," Nancy said. "Plus I want to show them the glove I found by the stuffed fox. I think I hear their voices downstairs. Let's go." She put the glove in her skirt pocket.

The two girls headed downstairs. They found Laura and her mother in the den, drinking iced tea.

"We made a big discovery," Nancy announced. "I have a feeling it's an important clue." She and George showed Morning Glory's snapshot to the Passanos and told them about finding it in Peter Greenbriar's desk drawer.

"Do you recognize this photo, Laura?" Nancy asked, settling on the sofa as Mrs. Passano poured her a glass of iced tea.

Gazing at the photograph, Laura grew pale. "It's Morning Glory, all right," she answered, "but I don't recognize this photo." She paused, then asked, "What—what do you think this means, Nancy?"

"I'm not sure," Nancy said. "But I think you

ought to watch him during feeding time for the next few days."

"Yes," Laura said. "Maybe Peter and I can take turns." She handed the snapshot back to Nancy, then slumped back listlessly in her chair.

"But are you sure you trust him?" Nancy had to ask. "After all, I found the photo in his desk drawer."

"Peter doesn't need a photo to recognize Morning Glory," Mrs. Passano said. "He made a terrible mistake mixing up the two horses' feed. But I still think the man is innocent."

"I do, too," Laura said firmly, sitting up straight. "He takes his job seriously. I can't imagine him wanting to hurt Morning Glory—or any horse, for that matter."

Mrs. Passano nodded in agreement. "What if Peter found the photograph somewhere else and just put it in his drawer?" she asked.

"Then why didn't he mention it to anyone?" George countered.

"Perhaps he thought it had just fallen out of a file," Mrs. Passano replied.

"I promise I'll question him about the snapshot later," Nancy agreed. "I'm not jumping to any conclusions right now. There are just too many possibilities."

Briefly, she went on to tell Laura and her mother her theory about the photo being used by a stranger to identify Morning Glory. She didn't mention that she thought the animal activists might be involved. She knew that the Mill River riders were already angry with Mark Plonsky and his friends. Until she had proof, she didn't want to add to the hostility.

"By the way," Nancy went on, holding out the brown leather glove, "I found this near the stuffed fox today. The tag inside says Marburg's Saddlery Shop. Do you know the store?"

"Oh, yes," Mrs. Passano said. "It's an old-fashioned saddlery in downtown Baltimore. They've been selling horse equipment and riding apparel for years."

"Just about everyone who hunts around here has shopped at Marburg's," Laura added as she checked out the glove. "It's not much of a clue. I wish I could say that I recognize this glove, but I don't."

"It's possible that a rider simply lost the glove during the hunt today," Mrs. Passano pointed out. "Maybe someone took it off while adjusting a saddle strap or something like that."

"Or it could have fallen out of a rider's pocket," Nancy said. "Still, I like to follow all leads—even if they seem like long shots."

"Well, it's just about feeding time," Mrs. Passano declared, handing the glove back to Nancy. "Why don't you girls go up to the stables and make sure Morning Glory's safe? I went out before the morning feeding and asked Peter to pay special attention to the feed—to make sure it was untainted."

The three girls trooped out to the barn in silence, each one worried about Morning Glory. Inside, Peter Greenbriar was carrying buckets of feed to the various stalls. Horses nickered and bobbed their heads, anticipating their dinner.

While Laura and George went to check on Morning Glory, Nancy followed Peter Greenbriar into the feed room. "Excuse me," she said, while the groom scooped feed into a bucket. "Can I ask you a few questions?"

He straightened up and said, "I'm really very busy, as you can see, miss."

"I understand, but it won't take more than a minute or two," Nancy said pleasantly. She took the snapshot of Morning Glory from her skirt pocket. "Do you recognize this photograph?"

The groom started. "Why, it's Morning Glory!"

"Yes, but do you recognize this particular photograph?" Nancy asked.

Greenbriar looked at Nancy suspiciously, his eyes narrowing. "I've never seen this photo, miss, if that's your question. But why are you asking?"

"I was looking in your desk drawer for a pen, and I found this," Nancy explained. "See? It has a spot of glue on the back, with a few grains of what looks like Taberol on it." Nancy showed him the back of the photo, hoping to startle him into telling her the truth.

"I don't know anything about this," the groom said. "Someone must have left it in my desk drawer." He stared at the floor, his face twitching slightly.

"Did you by any chance lose a glove?" Nancy pressed him.

"I don't think so," he said. "But I told you, I can't talk now. I'm busy—very busy."

Nancy gave a shrug. "I thought you wanted to help the Passanos find out who poisoned Dundee," she said.

"I—I don't know who did it," the groom stammered, heading toward the door. "So sorry. Got to feed the horses."

Nancy watched as he hurried out of the room with a clatter of feed buckets. Why is he being so evasive? she asked herself. Instinctively, she knew that Peter Greenbriar was hiding something. But what?

"Nancy, George," Mrs. Passano said the next morning as the two girls joined her in the kitchen. She handed them plates of homemade waffles. "Laura just went to help Peter bring the horses in from the pasture. She thought you might like to go on a trail ride with her later this morning. It will certainly be more relaxing than yesterday's hunt."

Nancy and George laughed. "Skydiving would

be more relaxing than yesterday's hunt," George joked, rubbing her leg, which was still sore from the fall she'd taken the day before.

"A trail ride sounds great, Mrs. Passano," Nancy said brightly.

After finishing breakfast, Nancy and George headed up to the barn to see if they could help out before they changed for the trail ride. It looked like it was going to be another gorgeous, sunny fall day, Nancy thought. She felt her spirits lift at the prospect of a good cross-country ride without having to chase a fox.

But as they neared the barn, they saw Laura running from the direction of the pasture, her long mahogany brown hair flying around her shoulders. Peter was behind her.

Nancy caught her breath. Something was wrong, she realized, terribly wrong. Her heart pounding, she sprinted toward Laura.

"Nancy, George!" Laura shouted, her face tight with fear. "Morning Glory's gone! My beautiful horse is gone!"

7

Something Crops Up

Nancy felt stunned. "Morning Glory disappeared from his stall?" she asked.

"No, from the pasture," Laura wailed. She began to sob. "Ask—ask Peter to tell you." With trembling hands, she wiped away tears from her eyes, only to have more gush out. "I have to tell Mom."

Without waiting for Nancy's response, Laura dashed frantically toward the house.

"We'll meet you at the barn," George called out after Laura.

"This is terrible!" Nancy exclaimed as she and George hurried toward Peter Greenbriar. "We have to find Morning Glory, and find him fast."

"This has nothing to do with me," the groom said, before Nancy could say anything. He turned toward the barn. "Follow me," he added.

Nancy and George followed him inside to Morning Glory's empty stall. "See?" Greenbriar said, waving a hand at a piece of paper tacked onto the door of the stall.

"What's that?" Nancy asked.

"A note from whoever stole Morning Glory," the groom said.

Nancy bent down to get a closer look. Pasted onto a white sheet of paper were letters cut out from a magazine: "Disband the Mill River Hunt, or you'll never see Morning Glory again."

"This is terrible!" George gasped.

Just then Mrs. Passano rushed into the barn, with Laura close behind her.

"Look at this," Nancy said grimly, pointing at the note. She felt sorry for Laura and her mother as they read the threatening message. First the poisoning, then the hunt sabotage, now this— how painful all this must be for them!

"Who would do this?" Laura cried.

"I can't believe someone would take Morning Glory hostage, just to force the hunt to meet their demands," Mrs. Passano said angrily.

"Well," Nancy said, "one thing's clear. Now we know that the problems at Sky Meadow Farm and the problems at the Mill River Hunt are related."

"Yes," Mrs. Passano said, "but who would want the hunt to disband?"

"Mark Plonsky!" Laura exclaimed. "It must be him. Who else would care?"

"I don't think we can automatically blame the animal activists," Nancy said, though the same thought had crossed her mind. "They certainly have reasons for wanting the hunt to break up. But we have no solid proof. I think we need to investigate all possible leads before pointing a finger at them."

"What leads?" Laura said dejectedly. "There are none."

Nancy turned to Peter Greenbriar. "Why weren't the horses in the barn last night?" she asked.

"It was a warm night, so after their evening feeding, I let them graze in the pasture. This morning, I discovered the note. I went out to the pasture. But Morning Glory wasn't there. That's when Laura found me."

"Did you hear anything unusual during the night?" Mrs. Passano asked.

"No," the groom replied. "I was in my apartment all night, but I didn't hear anything. And I swear I had nothing to do with Morning Glory's disappearance."

"Peter," Mrs. Passano said, "no one has accused you. We're just trying to find out some facts. Please don't let these questions upset you."

Mrs. Passano might not be suspicious of Peter Greenbriar, Nancy thought, but *she* was. The Passanos had only Peter Greenbriar's word that he was innocent. He could easily have taken the horse in the middle of the night. He was right there.

But why would he do such a thing? And why would he want the hunt to disband? Did he have some grudge against the Passanos? She was determined to find out.

Nancy stepped over to Laura and put her arm around her shoulders. "Laura, don't worry," she said. "I'm going to find Morning Glory and get to the bottom of the hunt sabotage."

"Thanks, Nancy," Laura said, her voice choked with tears. "You're a real friend."

Turning to Mrs. Passano, Nancy added, "I think you should report Morning Glory's disappearance to the police as soon as possible. After all, we're dealing with theft now."

"Thank you for reminding me, Nancy," Mrs. Passano said with a start. "I'll call right away from the stable." Mrs. Passano ducked into Peter Greenbriar's office to make the call.

"I have to start bringing the horses in for their feeding," the groom said, and he disappeared outside.

About fifteen minutes later, a young police officer with sandy-colored hair and freckles appeared at the barn door. After introducing himself as Officer McDonnell, he asked Mrs. Passano to explain what had happened. While she told him the story, he studied the note, which was still tacked onto Morning Glory's stall door. Then he glanced around uncertainly at the assembled group.

"I'll take the note down to police headquarters and show it to the chief," he said, "and I'll write up a report. But we're a small police department, and we don't have the manpower to investigate these kinds of pranks."

"But my horse was *stolen*," Laura said. "It's not a prank."

"Can we do anything in the meantime to speed along the investigation?" George cut in.

"Call your neighbors—spread the word," Officer McDonnell replied. "Somebody may have seen the horse."

He took the note off the door, then turned and strolled out of the barn. Nancy noted that he hadn't even bothered to wear gloves. Now his fingerprints would be all over the note.

"Some help he is," Laura scoffed after Officer McDonnell had driven away.

"He certainly doesn't seem very experienced," Mrs. Passano agreed. After a pause, she added, "I must tell the other board members of the hunt about this threat. It couldn't have come at a worse time—Opening Day's on Saturday. That's two days away!"

"Maybe I'll go down to the pasture," Nancy suggested, "and take a look around."

"You won't find anything out of whack down there," Peter Greenbriar declared as he walked by carrying two feed buckets. "I looked the place over thoroughly."

"Well, another pair of eyes might turn up something," George said. "Come to think of it," she added, turning toward Nancy, "I'll go with you."

Nancy and George headed out to the adjoining pasture from a side door of the barn. The large grassy field stretched all the way down the hill to the road far below, skirting the house on the right.

"The thief could have been seen from the house," George observed, "if someone had been awake. That's pretty daring, to kidnap a valuable horse from right outside his owners' windows."

Nancy studied the pasture's layout. The fence around the field had a gate in the far corner, near where the driveway and road intersected.

"Someone could have taken Morning Glory from that far gate," she suggested. "That way, the thief wouldn't have to drive the trailer up to the house and risk being heard."

"Or worry about hooves clopping on the driveway," George put in.

Nancy nodded. "Once Morning Glory was inside a trailer," she suggested, "the thief could have sneaked back to the barn and tacked the note on the stall door."

"Presuming the thief used a trailer and not a forest path," George pointed out. She idly kicked at the grass with the toe of her shoe. Then she froze. "Nancy, look!"

George stooped down and fished in the grass. Then she stood up, holding a long brown leather stick with a thick handle.

"It's a riding crop," Nancy declared. "And it looks like someone's initials are engraved on the handle."

"CJ?" George said, peering closely at the handle. "Who could that be?"

"I don't know," Nancy said. "But let's go find out."

The two girls jogged back to the barn. They found Laura and her mother talking to Peter Greenbriar.

"Does this belong to anyone you know?" Nancy asked, showing the Passanos the crop with its initials. "George and I found it in the pasture."

Peering closely at the crop, Laura and Mrs. Passano shook their heads.

But just then Nancy glanced at Peter Greenbriar. His face was deadly pale as he stared in silence at the riding crop.

8

Shopping for Leads

"Wait a minute!" Laura exclaimed. "CJ—could that be Charles Jackson's crop?"

"Charles Jackson?" Nancy remembered the name. Laura had said that Peter Greenbriar once worked for him. Was that why the groom looked so upset?

"I overheard a conversation about him at the hunt yesterday," she mentioned. "Some riders said that he was starting up his own hunt."

"That's right," Mrs. Passano said with a sigh. "Charles used to be a big supporter of Mill River. But after Cameron Shaw died, Charles and I both wanted to be master of the hounds. When I got appointed, he was miffed."

"Miffed is putting it mildly," Laura declared. "He stormed off to start up his new hunt, the Cold Spring Hounds."

"Sounds like he has a bit of a temper," George said dryly.

"That's for sure," Laura said. "He's a successful businessman, so he's used to getting his way. He's the type who works hard and plays hard."

"And his new hunt isn't a success?" Nancy asked.

"So far it's a flop," Laura said bluntly. "But to be fair, the Cold Spring Hounds is only in its first season. Not too many people know about it. Mill River is more than a hundred years old."

"If Mill River becomes a drag hunt," Mrs. Passano said, "Charles will be happy that he left. He's totally in favor of live fox hunting. In fact, that's why I was made master of the hounds. The riders who are in favor of having a drag hunt voted me in. They knew that Charles would have insisted on doing things the traditional way."

"Mr. Jackson certainly has a motive for wanting to wipe out Mill River," George said.

Mrs. Passano turned to the groom. "Peter, have you ever seen this crop before?" she asked. "You used to work for Charles. I thought you might recognize it."

For a moment the groom said nothing. Then his eyes met Mrs. Passano's. "The crop is mine, not Mr. Jackson's," he announced. "Mr. Jackson gave me the crop last year, along with a helmet and some other stuff from his barn. He was clearing it out before remodeling. The crop's definitely mine. That lets Mr. Jackson off the hook."

"Mr. Jackson may not have dropped the crop when Morning Glory was taken," Nancy pointed out. "Still, he has a powerful motive to want the Mill River Hunt to end. He could still have taken the horse." She turned to Peter Greenbriar. "Why did you quit as Mr. Jackson's groom?" she asked.

"The Passanos offered me a little more money," he replied.

"So how did your crop get in the pasture?" George asked.

"The crop proves nothing!" he declared. "I must have dropped it in the pasture a couple of days ago."

Mrs. Passano sighed deeply, then said, "You're right, Peter. It doesn't prove a thing."

Back at the house, Laura announced that she wanted to spend the morning making phone calls to neighbors about Morning Glory. After getting her address book from her room, she went into the den.

Mrs. Passano told Nancy and George that she planned to spend the day at the Mill River clubhouse. She needed to make sure that everything was in order for the Hunt Ball, which would be held the next night, on the eve of Opening Day.

"You're welcome to come by later and look

through the Mill River files for any leads," she suggested to Nancy and George as she picked up her keys and purse from a table in the front hallway.

"Thanks," Nancy said. "That's a great idea— since it's clear that the hunt sabotage and the horsenapping are linked. Can we meet you there after lunch?"

"Absolutely. See you then." With a quick wave, Mrs. Passano hurried out the front door.

"George," Nancy said, "there's one other lead I'd like to investigate before we meet with Mrs. Passano. Let's go to Marburg's Saddlery Shop and show them the leather glove I found. I know it's a long shot, but maybe they can identify its owner."

"Good idea, Nan," George said.

Nancy shrugged. "I hope so," she said. "We could really use a break. I'm getting frustrated. So far, every clue we've found seems to lead nowhere—the glove, the snapshot, the crop . . ."

"Well, don't give up on the glove yet," George said cheerfully. "And while we're at the shop, maybe we can explore a little of Baltimore. With all these weird things happening at the farm and on the hunt, I'm certainly up for a change of scene."

Nancy and George got directions to Marburg's from Laura. Then they headed for Baltimore in Nancy's blue Mustang.

Laura had suggested that they might want to look around Harborplace, two shopping pavilions built right on the Baltimore harbor. "Why don't we have an early lunch at Harborplace before we hit Marburg's?" Nancy suggested once they reached Baltimore. "Laura told me the store doesn't open till noon. If we can find an outdoor café, we could still enjoy this gorgeous weather."

"Sounds great," George said. "It'll make up for the fact that we didn't get to go riding this morning."

A few minutes later, George said, "That must be Harborplace, over to the right. Look—you can see the water and a lot of boats."

After parking the car, the two girls set off toward the shopping pavilions. They quickly found an outdoor café and sat down at a table shaded by a festive-looking umbrella. Menus had already been placed on the table. George immediately picked one up. "I'm hungry."

"Me, too," Nancy said.

A few minutes later, a waiter arrived to take their orders.

"I'd like a hamburger and an iced tea," George said.

"And I'd like the chicken salad special and a lime seltzer, please," Nancy said, handing the waiter her menu.

While the girls ate lunch, they talked about the case. "I suppose Mark Plonsky has the most obvious reason for wanting to wipe out the hunt," George said. "But I still can't believe that an animal activist would poison a horse."

"We can't rule him out, though. And we can't be blinded by the fact that we sympathize with his cause," Nancy warned her friend.

"You're right," George said. She took a sip of her iced tea, then added, "Well, speaking of motives, don't forget Charles Jackson. And it's clear that Peter Greenbriar is still loyal to him. Could they be working together?"

"That crossed my mind," Nancy said, frowning.

"But there's still the problem with the photograph," George reminded her. "Peter Greenbriar wouldn't need it."

"None of the clues seem to fit together," Nancy said. "Let's just hope we find some answers at Marburg's."

After lunch, they strolled back to the car and drove over to Fells Point, where they found Marburg's Saddlery Shop along a quaint cobblestoned street. After parking, Nancy and George got out of the car and walked over to the shop.

As Nancy pushed open the glass-paned wooden door, a bell hanging on the inside made a tinkling sound. Then the smell of leather and saddle soap hit her.

71

Marburg's was filled with saddles, bridles, and riding apparel. Odds and ends—brushes, curry combs, and cans of saddle soap—were tossed here and there in baskets. Nothing seemed organized. In fact, Nancy thought, it appeared that the merchandise hadn't been rearranged in years.

"Wow," George said, looking around at the overflowing shelves. "It's like entering another world."

An elderly man was sitting behind an antique cash register. Taking the glove from her pocket, Nancy went up to him and asked if he remembered who had bought it.

"No, miss, I'm sorry," he replied in a gravelly voice as he peered at the glove. "I carried this glove a couple of years ago but not recently. I couldn't possibly remember who bought it."

"Can you tell me what the size is?" Nancy asked.

The man put on a pair of wire-rimmed glasses and studied the glove. "Looks to me like a man's small," he judged. Nancy thanked the man and put the glove back in her pocket.

As she turned to leave, she noticed two young women sifting through a rack of riding jackets. The girls were whispering intensely. Curious, Nancy edged closer. She recognized one of the girls—Alexa Shaw's friend from the cub hunt. The other one was a stranger.

Suddenly, Alexa's friend whirled angrily toward the other girl. "You're wrong!" she cried. "She'd never do that!"

"You've got to admit it," the other girl insisted. "Alexa Shaw's just nuts about Morning Glory. She's the one who stole him—for sure!"

9

Wired for Danger

Nancy couldn't believe what she'd heard the girl say. Had Alexa Shaw stolen Morning Glory?

"I'll be right back," Nancy said to George. She walked over to where the two young women were standing. "Hi," she said with a friendly smile to the auburn-haired girl. "I spoke to you yesterday at the cub hunt. I'm Nancy Drew, a friend of Laura Passano's."

"Yes, I remember you," the girl said, looking surprised to see Nancy suddenly appear. She frowned at her friend, then turned back to Nancy. "I'm Isabel Hathaway, and this is my friend Lili Tsao."

"Nice to meet you both." Nancy paused. "Hathaway. Are you related to Grant Hathaway, the huntsman with Mill River?"

Isabel nodded. "He's my father," she ex-

74

plained. "We've known the Passanos for years. Laura called me this morning to tell me about Morning Glory's disappearance. I'm so sorry."

"Yes," Lili put in. "Isabel just told me about it. What a terrible thing to happen!"

"It sure is," Nancy agreed. "You can imagine how upset Laura is." Looking at Lili, Nancy asked, "I couldn't help overhearing—do you really think Alexa Shaw stole him?"

Isabel cut in before Lili could respond. "Alexa was furious when Laura outbid her in the auction, but I *know* my friend is no thief."

"You're right, Isabel," Lili agreed. "I shouldn't have said that. It's just that everyone knows how much Alexa wanted that horse."

So Alexa *had* coveted Morning Glory, Nancy mused, just as Laura said. Did Alexa want him badly enough to steal him—then write the note to throw blame on the animal activists? Alexa hadn't shown up at the hunt, Nancy remembered. Was that because she knew about the booby traps? Nancy's mind churned with questions as she listened to Lili and Isabel.

After saying goodbye to the girls, Nancy looked around for George. She found her trying on leather gloves at the counter.

"These would come in handy even if you're not a rider," George remarked as she handed the gloves back to the elderly store owner. "You could wear them out hiking in the woods, for instance."

"That's right, miss," he said. "They're great all-purpose outdoor gloves."

After thanking him, Nancy and George returned to the car. Nancy told George what she'd overheard in Marburg's.

"Alexa Shaw," George said thoughtfully as she put on her seat belt. "I wouldn't be surprised if she's behind everything. You've got to admit—she doesn't seem like a very nice person."

"But that doesn't mean she committed a crime," Nancy said. "Still, we'll have to check her out." She considered their next move. "What about searching Alexa's barn?" she suggested. "If she did steal Morning Glory, that's about the last place she'd take him. But we might find some evidence telling us where he is or about the poisoning."

"What about Charles Jackson?" George asked, as Nancy started the Mustang. "We should search his barn, too."

"Absolutely," Nancy said. "And I think it's time we poked around Mark Plonsky's house. We're bound to come up with something at one of those places. We have to hurry—Opening Day is almost here."

"Speaking of Opening Day," George said, checking her watch, "let's get on to the Mill River Hunt's offices. Mrs. Passano is expecting us."

Back in the country, Nancy and George followed Mrs. Passano's directions to the headquarters of the Mill River Hunt. Nancy drove up a long, tree-lined driveway, then parked under a majestic maple tree beside a spacious old brick farmhouse.

"What a great place for offices," George commented, as the two girls got out of the car. "I could work here."

Nancy laughed. "It's too beautiful, George. How could you concentrate? Besides, Laura told me it's not only used for Mill River's offices—it's also a clubhouse for their social events. And the fox hounds are kept here." Nancy pointed to an outdoor kennel. They could hear the friendly hounds yapping.

The front door was open, and Nancy and George entered. They immediately spotted Mrs. Passano, coming out of an office. "I'm so glad you're here, girls," she said when she saw them. "Laura just called me from home. She's completely distraught. No one she's talked to has seen Morning Glory. And I hate to think of what Opening Day will be like if . . ." Her voice trailed off.

"Don't worry, Mrs. Passano," Nancy said soothingly. "I just know we'll find Morning Glory and save the Mill River Hunt." Privately, Nancy wished she felt that confident. But all she could do was keep investigating—and hope for a break.

Inside the house, people were hurrying around, rearranging furniture, polishing silver, and scrubbing floors. "We're getting the place in order for the Hunt Ball tomorrow evening," Mrs. Passano explained.

"Where shall I put these, please?" a big, ruddy-faced man asked. He was carrying two large baskets of chrysanthemums.

"Ah, the flower arrangements have arrived!" Mrs. Passano exclaimed. "Let me show you where they go."

Nancy and George followed as Mrs. Passano led the florist down the center hallway lined with fox hunting prints. She stopped at the open back door. Outside, they could see a large yellow- and white-striped tent all set up for the party. "There's a long table in the tent. Just put them there," Mrs. Passano told the man with a sweep of her hand.

"Now, Nancy and George, let me show you our files." Mrs. Passano turned and led the girls into a nearby room. Two empty desks stood in the center, and a stack of file cabinets lined the back wall.

"Please help yourselves to anything you need here," Laura's mother said. "Don't worry if the phone rings. We'll let the machine pick up any calls."

"Thanks," Nancy said. Mrs. Passano hurried out. Turning to George, Nancy said, "Why don't you take from A through M? I'll do N through Z."

As quickly as they could, Nancy and George pored through thick files of correspondence and legal papers.

Looking up from a file marked General, George said, "This is interesting, Nan—a letter written by Cameron Shaw to Grant Hathaway about a year ago. Looks like Mr. Shaw was worried because a local farm was sold to a developer. He promises Mr. Hathaway to do what he can to preserve the countryside from development."

Nancy frowned. "How could that tie in with the hunt sabotage?"

"I'm not sure," George admitted in a discouraged tone. "Unless . . . what if a developer is trying to ruin the hunt to get the land?"

"I doubt it," Nancy said. "This crime seems so personal—like there's someone who bears a grudge for some reason."

"Well, I haven't found anything else," George said with a sigh. "I even went through these old newspapers. Nothing."

"I haven't found anything, either," Nancy said, putting away a file. "But don't worry. I have a feeling we'll get more answers at Charles Jackson's."

After closing the file cabinets, Nancy and George went to find Mrs. Passano to ask her for directions to Mr. Jackson's horse farm. It turned out to be only a short drive away.

As Nancy steered her Mustang up his driveway, a charming white Victorian house with green shutters loomed up behind an evergreen hedge. A brick walkway led to the front door.

Parking in the turnaround, Nancy noticed a barn and two other outbuildings clustered near a large pasture. Hanging on the door of one outbuilding, a hand-lettered sign said The Cold Spring Hounds—Office. They got out of the car and headed that way.

"Let's see if anyone's around first. I don't want to get caught snooping," Nancy said.

She rapped on the office door. "Come in," a voice boomed.

Opening the door, Nancy saw a middle-aged African American man with salt-and-pepper hair rummaging through paper on a desk. Glancing around the office, she noticed that there were no files, no normal office clutter.

"Hello," the man said, jumping up. "I'm Charles Jackson, master of the Cold Spring Hounds. Are you here to join my new hunt?"

As he shook her hand, Nancy checked his hands. They were small, despite his stocky frame. Small enough to fit into the glove from Marburg's?

"It's nice to meet you, Mr. Jackson," Nancy said, smiling back at him. "I'm Nancy Drew, and this is George Fayne. We'd love to join your hunt, but I'm afraid we're just visiting in this area." She looked over at George and said, "We love to ride, though, and we heard you were starting a new hunt. We thought we'd stop by to check it out, in case we ever decide to move here."

"Well, I tell you," Mr. Jackson said, "one outing

with my hunt, and you'll definitely want to move here."

Nancy had to smile. "I'm sure you're right."

"When does your hunt go out next?" George asked.

"Our Opening Day is four days from now," Mr. Jackson replied, his face glowing with excitement. He paused, then added snidely, "Of course, I wouldn't want it to fall on Mill River's big day."

"Too bad—we won't be here in four days," Nancy said. "We're leaving the Passanos' before that." She waited for his response.

"The Passanos? Is that who you're visiting?" Mr. Jackson glowered at them. "Well, of course, they'll try to get you to hunt with Mill River, but don't listen to them. I have permission to hunt over even more beautiful countryside, farther out." He gestured grandly.

"But aren't you friendly with the Passanos?" Nancy asked innocently. "I found a riding crop in their field with your initials on it."

"A riding crop with *my* initials in *their* field?" he repeated, looking incredulous. "Hmmm. Maybe it's one I gave my former groom, Peter Greenbriar. He works over there now."

So Peter Greenbriar's story checked out, Nancy thought—provided Charles Jackson was telling the truth.

"Well," Nancy said, "I'm sorry we won't be able to hunt with you. Maybe another time."

"While you're here, though, can I show you my new horses?" Mr. Jackson offered, moving around the desk. "Anyone with an interest in riding should really see them. They're gorgeous animals. I keep them in the far pasture—better grass there."

This was the chance Nancy had been waiting for. "We'd love to see them," she said promptly. The two girls followed the horse breeder out of his office and toward the pasture.

As they passed the barn, Nancy suddenly stopped and opened her shoulder bag. "Oh, no!" she exclaimed. "My sunglasses aren't in my bag." She turned to Mr. Jackson. "I probably left them in the car. You two go on ahead. I'll catch up."

Nancy gave George a meaningful glance, and George immediately began asking Mr. Jackson questions.

As soon as George and Mr. Jackson were out of sight, Nancy headed into the barn. Parked inside was a Land Rover, its sides splattered with mud. She walked by it and went into the feed room. Quickly, she checked to see if there were any bags of Taberol. She found nothing. She also found nothing out of order in the tack room. She wanted to take a look in Mr. Jackson's office. But first, she decided to check out the Land Rover.

Peeking into the front seat, all Nancy saw were music tapes scattered on the floor. She craned her neck to look into the backseat.

Nancy caught her breath. There, shoved between the front and back seats, were wire cutters and a shiny coil of barbed wire—just like the wire that had been run along the fence rail the morning of the cub hunt!

At that moment Nancy heard footsteps approaching the side door. Mr. Jackson! she thought. Frantically, she looked around for a place to hide.

Suddenly, the door burst open.

There stood Peter Greenbriar, glaring at her.

10

A Very Sharp Note

Peter Greenbriar hovered in the open doorway. "Hello, Miss Drew," he said, his blue eyes glittering icily. "I didn't expect to find *you* here."

"No," Nancy said guardedly. "It's a surprise for us both." Thinking quickly, she added, "George and I are here to look at Mr. Jackson's horses—to purchase one, maybe." She smiled, hoping he'd buy her excuse.

"Surely there aren't any horses inside the Land Rover," Peter Greenbriar said with a sarcastic chuckle.

"I thought I'd left something in it," Nancy said, bluffing. "We all rode out in it earlier to look at the horses. They're in the far pasture."

"Is that right?" the groom replied, raising his eyebrows.

Nancy couldn't tell whether he believed her or

84

not, but she decided to take the offensive. "And why are *you* here?" she asked.

"I stopped by to ask Mr. Jackson whether he might have seen Morning Glory. But he's not in the house or in the office, and I need to get going. Will you ask him for me?"

"Yes, sure," Nancy said.

"Well, then, I'll be seeing you." The groom pursed his lips and stared at Nancy for a moment. Then he turned around and left.

Nancy paused, taking stock of the situation. Could Peter Greenbriar have had some other reason for stopping by? Maybe to plot with Charles Jackson about ways to make the Mill River Hunt disband?

As she left the barn, Nancy saw the brake lights of a car flash as it retreated down the driveway—Peter Greenbriar's car, she guessed. She turned and spotted George and Mr. Jackson closing the gate to a nearby pasture.

"Hi there, Miss Drew," Mr. Jackson said as he approached her. "Where have you been all this time? I've already shown George my best horses."

"I've been searching my car for my sunglasses," Nancy said quickly. "We'd better be going, George," she added. "We're supposed to stop by the Shaws' later."

"That's right. I'm glad you reminded me. Let's go," George said, taking her cue from Nancy.

"Thanks, Mr. Jackson, for showing me your hunters."

"You can always count on Cold Spring to have the best hunters around," Mr. Jackson said. "But did I hear you mention the Shaws? You could walk there, through the woodland trails. Our farms are adjacent."

"If we had more time, that would be great," Nancy said. "But we're kind of late."

"Fine," Mr. Jackson said. "The Shaws live just down White Rock Road, the same road I'm on. Theirs is the next driveway."

Waving goodbye, Nancy and George climbed into the Mustang and set off for the Shaws'. As Nancy pulled onto the main road, she told George about finding the barbed wire in Mr. Jackson's car and about Peter Greenbriar's surprise visit.

"Whew!" George exclaimed. "Lucky it wasn't Mr. Jackson who found you."

"You're telling me," Nancy said. "It was a close call."

"But surely Peter Greenbriar guessed you were investigating," George pointed out. "What if he tells Mr. Jackson anyway?"

"I'll deal with it then." Nancy shuddered. "Mr. Jackson has a nice manner on the outside, but I bet he can get pretty angry. Look at how mad he is at Mill River." She paused, then said, "But at least he told us where Alexa lives. I didn't want to ask

Mrs. Passano. I didn't want her to know we were checking out her friend's daughter."

The two girls drove in silence as Nancy concentrated on finding the Shaws' driveway. She spotted it around a bend, turned the car in, and headed up to a cream-colored stucco house with black shutters, surrounded by large boxwoods.

Nancy pulled up next to a small gray sedan. At that moment, the front door of the house opened, and Alexa's mother stepped outside. Dressed in a madras skirt and a straw hat, she was carrying two pies.

Mrs. Shaw gave Nancy and George a friendly nod as they climbed out of their car. "Hello, girls," she said. "I'm sorry I can't shake hands, but I'm laden down with these pies. Alexa and I made half a dozen, from our apple trees out back. I'm taking these two over to a neighbor." She set one on the hood of her car to get a free hand to open the car door.

"That's okay, Mrs. Shaw," Nancy said with a smile. "We're just looking for Alexa." Suddenly, she remembered something Alexa had said the day before. "Yesterday, Alexa asked to borrow a bridle from Mrs. Passano. Since we were in the area, we thought we'd pick it up if she's finished with it."

"I wonder why Alexa needed a bridle?" Mrs. Shaw said sharply. She halted and frowned. "We have dozens of our own. Oh, I hope she's not going to try to ride with the hunt on Opening Day. She knows how I feel about *that*." Her voice trembled, and she added fiercely, "I wish she'd give up riding altogether!"

Nancy was taken aback. She knew that Alexa was a skilled rider. Wasn't her mother being a little overprotective?

"Well, Alexa's inside," Mrs. Shaw went on, her voice still shaky. "I'm sure she'll be happy to see you." After carefully placing the pies in her car, Mrs. Shaw drove away.

"Wow," George commented. "I can't believe Mrs. Shaw is so upset about Alexa's riding. You'd think she would have accepted it by now. Especially since Alexa's dad was a big fox hunter, too. He was master of the hounds and everything."

"Maybe that's why Mrs. Shaw gets so worked up about it," Nancy said. "Remember, Cameron Shaw was killed during a hunt. And I gather Mrs. Shaw isn't much of a rider. She may ride now and then. But she doesn't have any attachment to the hunt."

"That's true," George admitted. "Still, what a drag for Alexa."

"Well, let's get on with our investigation," Nancy said, changing the subject. "Do you want to check out—"

Just then, out of the corner of her eye, Nancy thought she saw a shadow fall across the grass to the left of the house. When she looked over that way, though, it had disappeared.

"Did you see that?" George asked, grabbing Nancy's arm.

"Sure did," Nancy replied. "Wait right here."

Nancy inched quietly over to the corner of the house and peeked behind it. She was just in time to see a dark-haired man in a flannel shirt darting around the back wall.

Breaking into a soft jog, Nancy followed him behind the house. He disappeared around the far end. But from the hair color and the build, Nancy was sure the guy was Mark Plonsky.

"Stop!" Nancy shouted. She ran as fast as she could to catch up. In seconds she turned the corner, too, determined to find out what the man was doing. But to her surprise, no one was there.

Nancy glanced quickly at the side of the house. There were no doors, and all the window screens were shut. But a patch of woods skirted the house, and Nancy guessed the man had darted in there.

She dashed toward the front of the house, rounding the last corner. "Did you see anyone?" she asked George breathlessly, stopping at the front door.

"No," George said, looking puzzled.

Nancy told George about the man. "He must have ducked into the woods," she said. "They're just a few feet away from the side of the house."

"Did you recognize him at all?" George asked.

"I couldn't see him that well," Nancy admitted. "But it *might* have been Mark Plonsky. It clearly wasn't Peter Greenbriar or Charles Jackson. But what would he be doing at the Shaws'?"

"Maybe he was spying on *us*," George suggested.

"How could Mark even know we're here?" Nancy replied.

"Beats me," George said with a shrug.

Wearily, Nancy went to knock at the Shaws' door. After a long day of investigating, she felt hot, tired, and bedraggled. Next to Alexa, she thought, I'll probably look like a total mess.

Alexa opened the door, looking cool in khaki pants and a crisp white shirt. Her blond hair was held back with tortoiseshell combs.

Looking blankly at Nancy and George, Alexa said, "May I help you?"

Nancy and George exchanged glances. Is it possible she doesn't even recognize us? Nancy wondered.

"Hi, Alexa," she said. "I'm Nancy Drew, and this is George Fayne. We met you yesterday at the Passanos'."

"Oh, yes, now I remember," Alexa said, still not smiling.

"We were in the neighborhood and thought we could pick up the bridle you borrowed from the Passanos," Nancy said smoothly.

"It's in the tack room in the stable—it's marked

'Passano,' of course," Alexa said in a bored voice. She started to shut the door.

George swiftly blocked the door with her foot. "Would it be possible for me to get a glass of water?" she asked sweetly. "Nancy and I have been on the road all afternoon."

Alexa heaved a sigh. "There's some lemonade in the kitchen," she told them. She turned around and headed down a long hallway, not bothering to look back to see if her guests were following.

In the kitchen, George and Nancy poured themselves glasses of lemonade and sat on stools.

"We've been out all day, looking for Morning Glory," Nancy said innocently. She studied Alexa's face, hoping for a reaction. "Did Laura tell you he's missing?"

"Yes, she called me this morning—in tears," Alexa said, rolling her eyes. "I mean, shouldn't she try to calm down a little? For Morning Glory's sake? How can she look for him if she's so upset?"

Nancy set down her glass of lemonade, her hand shaking in anger. She couldn't believe Alexa's attitude. "I understand that you once felt strongly about Morning Glory, too," Nancy reminded the other girl.

"What exactly do you mean?" Alexa asked, glaring at Nancy.

"When Laura won Morning Glory at the auction, you must have been mad," Nancy said.

"No," Alexa said curtly. "Fair is fair. I didn't

have enough money, and Laura did. It's as simple as that." Alexa looked at Nancy stonily, as though daring her to ask any more questions about Morning Glory.

"Now, about that bridle," Alexa went on, standing up and motioning Nancy to the door. "As I said before, it's in the tack room in the barn—that large red building to the left of the house."

There was nothing to do but obey Alexa's not-so-subtle hints. Nancy and George headed for the barn. "She sure wanted to get rid of us," George said dryly.

"Yes, but it works to our advantage," Nancy said. "If she doesn't want to have anything to do with us, she won't pay much attention to where we go. We'll have a chance to investigate."

George nodded. "Still, she didn't have to be so rude. I feel sorry for Laura, being forced to play with Alexa when they were kids."

"Me, too," Nancy agreed.

After looking back to see that Alexa wasn't watching, the two girls quickly walked past the barn.

"George, I know it's a long shot, but why don't you search the paddock for clues, then pick up the bridle?" Nancy suggested. "At first, I thought it would be implausible that Alexa would bring the horse here if she stole it. But Mrs. Shaw seems to dislike horse riding so much that she probably wouldn't even notice if Morning Glory was in her field. So I'll check out the field and meet you back at the car."

"Okay," George said, then went off to the paddock.

Nancy climbed up a small hill to inspect the field. Morning Glory wasn't there. Nancy walked down to the field and spent ten minutes or so searching the ground. Finding nothing, she walked back to the stable. But just as she was about to go in, she heard a noise coming from the barn roof. She looked up.

A huge pitchfork was zooming down from the roof—pointing straight at her!

Nancy dashed under the eave of the barn. The pitchfork landed in the soft earth just inches from her feet, steel prongs quivering with the impact.

Nancy looked at it in horror and relief. Then she noticed a piece of white paper impaled upon one of the knife-sharp prongs.

With shaky fingers, Nancy bent forward to pick up the pitchfork and remove the paper.

It was a note, written in crude block letters: "Mind your own business, Blondie, or worse will happen!"

11

Horsing Around

Nancy looked up at the roof of the barn again. Who'd thrown that pitchfork at her? An inch closer, and she would have been badly hurt.

She didn't see anyone. Quickly, she ran around to the back of the barn. No one was on that side of the roof, either.

Glancing around, Nancy noticed that the woods stopped only a few feet from the back of the barn. Not only that, but the back roof sloped down to a small hill. Someone could have scrambled down and jumped the four feet from the roof to the grass.

Whoever threw the pitchfork, she though, must be hiding in those woods. Was it the same dark-haired man she'd seen sneaking around Alexa's house?

And was that man Mark Plonsky?

Nancy slipped the note that had been impaled on the pitchfork into her pocket. Just then she heard a thudding noise inside the barn. She caught her breath. What if she'd been wrong about the woods, and her attacker was hiding in the barn?

She decided to check inside, just in case. Nerves tingling with apprehension, she peered into the dim, cavernous space. If the person who'd thrown the pitchfork was hiding inside, Nancy knew she could get trapped. Calm down, Drew, she told herself. This is a piece of cake compared with some of your other cases.

Cautiously, Nancy entered the barn and glanced around, letting her eyes get accustomed to the barn's darkness. The Shaws' barn had fewer stalls than the Passanos'—only five or six—and it had a low hayloft. Was that where the pitchfork had come from?

Nancy climbed the ladder to the loft and looked around. Several bales of hay were stacked there, but otherwise nothing. From this vantage point, she could see the main part of the barn below her. Other than one horse peacefully munching hay, Nancy saw no signs of life there.

She examined the ceiling next but saw no evidence of a trap door. The thudding noise she'd heard must have been made by the horse, Nancy mused.

Discouraged, Nancy leaned out through a window in the hayloft. To the right, she saw George holding a bridle and craning her neck around—looking for her, Nancy guessed. Nancy scooted down from the loft and started out the barn door to join George. Suddenly, she came face-to-face with Alexa.

"Oh!" Nancy said, surprised. "Hi. I'm looking for George."

"She's right there," Alexa said, giving Nancy an odd look. She pointed in the direction of Nancy's car. "I was just talking to her. She's got the bridle."

What was Alexa doing at the barn? Nancy wondered. Could *she* have thrown the pitchfork? She would have had enough time to run up here after Nancy and George left her down at the Shaws' house. Even though Alexa seemed cool and calm, Nancy sensed the blond girl was good at putting up a front.

As though reading Nancy's thoughts, Alexa explained, "I'm here to check on my horse's leg. Unfortunately, she's still laid up. By the way," she went on, "as I was telling George, I put a pie in the backseat of your car. It's for the Passanos—from my mother."

"Thank you," Nancy said. "And thank your mom for us." Privately, Nancy wondered how someone as friendly as Mrs. Shaw could have a daughter as cold as Alexa.

Should she tell Alexa about the pitchfork? She

might as well, she decided. She was curious to see Alexa's reaction.

"How awful!" Alexa exclaimed after Nancy had told her. Her eyes were wide with horror.

Nancy was surprised. Alexa seemed genuinely concerned. Still, Nancy thought, Alexa might be a very good actress. If she was behind these pranks, she'd need to put on a pretty good acting job.

After a pause, Alexa said, "Maybe someone left the pitchfork on the roof by mistake. I'll have to talk to Eddie about that. He mows the lawn and does a little work around our stables."

"But why would he leave a pitchfork on the roof?" Nancy asked.

"Don't ask me," Alexa replied with a shrug.

Nancy debated whether to show Alexa the note stuck to the pitchfork, but she decided not to. If Alexa didn't know that Nancy was a detective, why give herself away by showing her the note?

After saying goodbye to Alexa, Nancy walked off to join George, who was now in the car. "Hi, Nan," George said. "Where have you been?"

"Dodging pitchforks," Nancy said, grinning as she opened the car door. Once inside, Nancy told George about the pitchfork and the note.

George looked anxiously at her friend. "It seems like this case is heating up. You'd better be careful, Nan."

"Don't worry, George, I'm always careful,"

Nancy said. "But I'm glad things *are* heating up. It means the culprit thinks we're onto something.

"The note tells us that he or she knows we're investigating this case," Nancy went on. "Peter Greenbriar is the only suspect who knows I'm a detective, but he could have told Charles Jackson. And Mr. Jackson knew we were coming over here. Remember, there's a shortcut through the woods between his property and the Shaws'. Either he or Peter Greenbriar could have followed us and thrown the pitchfork."

"But don't you think it was the dark-haired man you saw running off?" George asked.

"Possibly, but we have no proof," Nancy said. "I wonder if he overheard us talking about our investigation. We need to check Mark Plonsky's house anyway. But I don't know where he lives."

George glanced at her watch. "It's six o'clock already. The Passanos are expecting us for dinner."

Nancy sighed. "I guess you're right," she said. "We should go back to Sky Meadow. But I hate having to stop now. I feel like we're finally on a roll."

Back at Sky Meadow Farm, Nancy took a shower, then went downstairs to help Mrs. Passano set the table for dinner.

"Did you and George discover anything today?" Mrs. Passano asked hopefully.

Nancy frowned. She didn't want to tell Mrs.

Passano yet about the barbed w re in Mr. Jackson's car. She wanted more proof of his guilt first. And she didn't want to tell Mrs. Passano about the pitchfork attack, for fear she'd worry. Besides, she might tell Mrs. Shaw, her best friend, that Nancy had almost been injured. With Alexa now a suspect, Nancy didn't want Mrs. Shaw getting involved.

"George found some correspondence in the Mill River files," Nancy said. She told Mrs. Passano about Cameron Shaw's letter to Grant Hathaway.

"Cameron was always worried about the countryside getting too developed," Mrs. Passano explained. "He did buy up some local acreage for the hunt club shortly before he died. That land will always stay preserved. But most of the land we hunt over belongs to private owners. They could decide to sell it or build on it."

Nancy filed away that bit of information, though she still wasn't sure what it had to do with the sabotage.

Laura wandered into the dining room. Her eyes looked glazed. "It's getting dark already," she said in a dull voice. "Time for Morning Glory to eat. I sure hope whoever stole him is feeding him okay."

"Don't worry, Laura," Nancy said, putting an arm around her. "I've promised to find him, and I will. First thing tomorrow, I'd like to go to Mark Plonsky's house. Can you tell me where he lives?"

Laura frowned. "You won't find Morning Glory there—Mark doesn't have a barn. Though he could have hidden Morning Glory in the woods near his house." She looked thoughtfully out the window. "Mark lives in a riverside cottage, close to a forest trail. We could all ride over together." She managed a faint smile. "We can have a nice trail ride, just like I promised you guys—before all this horrible stuff happened."

I've just got to help Laura find her horse, Nancy thought. But how? She was running out of ideas—and time.

Soon after breakfast the next morning, the girls were on horseback, heading for Mark Plonsky's cottage. Laura, on her mom's horse Trimble, led the way.

"Laura," Nancy said as they rode abreast, "I'd like to know a little more about Mark Plonsky. Has he lived in this area long?"

"He moved here about a year and a half ago," Laura explained. "He started protesting the hunt last year, when Mr. Shaw was still the master."

"What does he do for a living?" George asked.

"He directs a local theater company," Laura replied.

"Really?" Nancy said, interested. "That stuffed fox looked so professional—like it was a theater prop or something."

"Well, there's no question Mark has a flair for

the dramatic," Laura said. "Actually, I think he might be a nice guy. But he never even tries to be friendly with anyone he knows is involved with fox hunting. He's pretty passionate about his beliefs."

The three girls came upon a large green meadow. Trimble began to dance with excitement. Laura let him break into a canter. "Don't let the horses go too fast," she called to Nancy and George. "There's a jump—a chicken coop—down on the far side of the hill. You don't want the horses heading into it out of control."

Behind Laura, Nancy urged on Hopscotch, while George and Lancelot brought up the rear. As she started down the hill behind Laura, Nancy leaned forward, eagerly anticipating the jump.

Suddenly, Lancelot bolted ahead and galloped headlong toward the jump. George frantically sawed on the reins. Nancy realized that Lancelot was totally out of control!

Nancy gasped as she saw Lancelot veering away from the jump and heading toward a thick pine grove. If George didn't stop him in time, she'd be whipped right into the dense thicket of trees!

Just then, as Lancelot neared the trees, a dark-haired man appeared ominously out of the woods.

It was Mark Plonsky.

12

George's Near Miss

Just before Lancelot crashed into the thicket, Nancy saw Mark Plonsky rush forward, holding his arms out wide in front of the horse. Lancelot pulled up sharply, and Mark Plonsky grabbed the bridle. Nancy sighed in relief, then exchanged looks with Laura.

"Whew, that was a close call," Laura said, her voice shaken. "What happened? Did Lancelot shy at something?"

"It looked like Lancelot just took off," Nancy replied. She pulled Hopscotch up next to Trimble, who had stopped obediently before the chicken coop. "Isn't it strange that Mark Plonsky would be lurking in the woods at the exact moment George needed him?" Nancy asked Laura in a low voice. Nancy looked down the hill, where George

102

seemed to have struck up a conversation with the handsome activist.

"How could he have known we'd be riding here?" Laura said. "I think it was just a coincidence. Come on—let's go over and see what's up."

The two girls guided their horses over to the edge of the woods. George, still on Lancelot, was thanking Mark Plonsky for coming to her rescue.

"It's lucky I happened to be out for my morning walk," he said. "I have an appointment at ten o'clock, but there's time for you to stop by my house for a cup of tea. To settle your nerves."

"I'm really fine," George said. "But I'd love some tea, anyway. As long as my friends can come, too, of course."

Glancing briefly at Nancy and Laura, he nodded. Then he started off down a woodland path, with Lancelot walking beside him.

"That's big of him to let us tag along," Nancy whispered dryly to Laura as they rode down the path.

Laura giggled. Then suddenly, she caught her breath.

"What's wrong?" Nancy asked.

"The bit on Lancelot's bridle," Laura murmured. "It's a snaffle. Why didn't I notice that before?"

"I guess because George saddled and bridled

Lancelot herself. I remember you saying that Lancelot needs a curb bit, though." Nancy frowned, puzzled by this new development.

"No wonder Lancelot ran away," Laura said, keeping her voice low. "He can barely feel a snaffle. He wouldn't even know George was trying to stop him." Laura paused, then added, "I wonder if someone swapped his bit intentionally."

Nancy considered the idea. Someone might have wanted to scare George—and Nancy along with her—off the case.

Could Mark have been spying on them this morning and seen them getting ready for the trail ride? Could he have found a way to get into the stable and swap the bit?

But Peter Greenbriar, she realized, was the likeliest suspect. He knew Lancelot needed a strong bit.

Then Laura said, "That was the bridle Alexa borrowed. She borrowed it because she wanted to try a curb bit on a horse she's training, and she didn't have one in her stable. But I'm positive the curb was on it when it was returned. I would've noticed otherwise."

Alexa? Nancy thought. She might well want to scare the girls off the case.

As Laura spoke, Nancy gazed down the path at George bending over Lancelot's neck, chatting with Mark Plonsky. George seemed to be getting along pretty well with the guy, Nancy observed.

She hoped George could get some information from him.

Before long, a tiny stone mill house came into view, and Nancy heard the sound of rushing water nearby. On the far side of the house, a dirt road led to a narrow wooden bridge. The road then snaked through the woodlands beyond. A river gushed underneath the bridge and eventually disappeared under a canopy of trees.

"Is this his house?" Nancy asked Laura.

Laura nodded. "There are several of these cute old houses scattered along the Mill River," she told Nancy. "The mill workers used to live in them two hundred years ago. The old mill is just a half mile upriver. It's not used anymore, but the waterfall next to it still turns its wheel."

After dismounting, the three girls took off their horses' bridles and put on halters they'd brought with them in Laura's backpack. After snapping lead ropes on the halters, they tied their horses to the fence surrounding the house, then followed Mark Plonsky inside. He led them to a sitting area by a fireplace. The sunlight filtering through the leaves outside made lively patterns on the braided rug.

Above the fireplace mantel were hand-painted placards reading Let the Fox Live and Stop the Senseless Slaughter, with pictures of happy fox faces painted in each corner. Nancy wondered if Mark had painted them himself.

After he brought in mugs of tea, Nancy told George about the swapped bit, glancing at him to see how he reacted to the news. He said nothing as he sank down on a corner of the sofa.

"I tried to reach you on the phone yesterday, Mark," Laura said. "I wanted to tell you that Morning Glory, my hunter, is missing."

"I overheard the news yesterday at the grocery store," Mark said matter-of-factly. "I'm sorry. I haven't seen him, though. Obviously, I would have called you if I had."

"Has your group made any headway with the board of the Mill River Hunt?" Nancy asked him.

"What do you mean?" he asked sharply, staring at Nancy in a challenging way.

"Are you persuading them to switch to a drag hunt?" Nancy replied, staring directly into his steel gray eyes, determined not to look away first.

"We *would* be making headway, except that we're being blamed for the sabotage at the cub hunt two days ago," Mark said coolly. "The board won't talk to me. I just hope the culprit is caught soon. Maybe the board will listen to me when they realize I'm not a saboteur."

"That's funny," Nancy countered. "I heard that *you* were the inflexible one—you went out and interfered with the hounds before you'd ever

106

discussed the issue with the board." Nancy continued to look at him, her gaze unflinching.

Mark Plonsky raised his eyebrows. "How flattering," he said sarcastically. "I seem to be the subject of everyone's gossip around here." He put his mug down on a side table. Then he stood up abruptly. "Well, it's true I didn't discuss my plans with the board beforehand. First I wanted to show the hunt that I meant business—and I succeeded."

"But have you won your real goal—to get Mill River to stop hunting foxes?" Nancy pointed out. "Or have you just made the riders more stubborn? And maybe even turned people against you who might agree with you?"

Leaning on the mantel, Mark sighed. "I have to admit my approach may have been too strong," he said. "But in any case, I'm willing to talk now."

"The board would talk to you if you could prove you're not trying to sabotage them," Laura told him.

"I had nothing to do with the barbed wire or the stuffed fox!" Mark declared. "I've told you that already."

"Calm down, Mark," George said gently.

Taking a deep breath, he sat down next to George on the sofa. "I'm planning to come to the Hunt Ball tonight, as a show of goodwill," he announced. "A guy I work with had an extra invitation—his wife can't go. I'm hoping the social setting will make the hunt diehards loosen up and be more willing to listen to me."

"I hope it works, for everyone's sake," George said. "But now, why don't you take us on that tour of your house you promised me?"

"By all means," Mark said politely. "Right this way."

As he led the girls on a quick tour of his cottage, Nancy lagged behind, scouting around for clues in the neat, spare rooms. She found nothing, not even any evidence of Mark's theatrical career. Nancy felt baffled. Of course, she reminded herself, there was nothing to prove he *didn't* take Morning Glory or sabotage the hunt, either.

After the tour, they all walked outside. Once on their horses, the girls said goodbye to Mark Plonsky. "I hope to see you at the ball tonight, George," Nancy heard him say in a low voice.

"You will," George murmured, smiling.

Nancy felt uneasy. Was Mark deliberately trying to charm George? If so, why? She had to admit that this visit had showed her another side of the guy. But she still wasn't sure she trusted him.

"Do you by any chance know the Shaws?" Nancy asked Mark, remembering the dark-haired man at their house yesterday.

"I know who they are," he replied offhandedly. "Cameron Shaw's widow and daughter. I'm sure his death has been sad for them. I don't know them well, though. Why?"

"I think I left something at their house yesterday," Nancy said. "I wondered if you knew the way there cross-country. I'd like to ride over now to get it."

Mark looked shrewdly at Nancy. "Laura knows the way. Ask her," he said. Waving goodbye, he turned around and went inside his house.

Nancy wondered if Mark suspected that her question had been a setup. Or was he trying to cover up the fact that he'd been lurking around there the day before?

Back at Sky Meadow Farm, the girls unsaddled the horses, rubbed them down, and then trooped down to the kitchen for a quick lunch. As Mrs. Passano sliced some tomatoes for sandwiches, she told them that she had called Officer McDonnell to check in with him about Morning Glory.

"He's not being very aggressive," she complained. "I had to ask to speak to his boss. The problem is that their office is understaffed, and they don't have many leads to go on."

"But they should be out looking for leads!" Laura said indignantly. "Anyone can see that Morning Glory was stolen. They should be checking roads and tollbooths. Morning Glory could be in another state by now."

109

"But, Laura, don't forget the note," Nancy reminded her. "It said he was stolen to force the Mill River Hunt to disband. I'll bet this is a local job, done by someone who bears a grudge toward the hunt—or toward your family. I just know Morning Glory is somewhere nearby—and I just know we'll find him soon."

"How do I look, Nan?" George asked, modeling her long red silk dress. George rarely got dressed up. She preferred sweatsuits or jeans to skirts and dresses.

"George, you look gorgeous!" Nancy exclaimed. "I love the way you've brushed back your hair. Your gold earrings look great, too."

Then she turned and backed up to George. "Could you zip me up?" Nancy's turquoise dress shimmered with tiny sequins. She was glad Laura had told them in advance that they'd be going to a ball. She never would have bought such a fancy dress otherwise.

"This is one great dress," George said. "You'll be the belle of the ball."

Nancy laughed as she adjusted the spaghetti straps. "No, George, I have a feeling that tonight is your night," she said. "Don't forget—Mark Plonsky will be there."

George blushed. "I hope his plan works and that he'll get a chance to talk to some of the hunt club members," she said. "But what if none of them will talk to him—who's he going to talk to all evening?"

"I can't imagine," Nancy said dryly, shooting George a teasing look.

Just then Laura called them from downstairs. The two girls hurried to join their friend. After complimenting one another on their dresses, they all set off for the Hunt Ball in Nancy's car. Nancy knew that Laura's mother had gone over earlier with Mr. Hathaway to take care of a number of last-minute details.

In a few minutes, Nancy pulled up to the Mill River clubhouse. Yellow lamplight blazed from every window, and Japanese lanterns swung between trees, lighting the way to the tent out back.

Peter Greenbriar, who was helping out in the parking lot, directed them to a parking spot. Nancy turned off the car and got out. "That's funny," she murmured to Laura. "That looks like Charles Jackson in the car right next to us. I thought he'd quit Mill River."

"Well, Mr. Jackson still has a lot of friends here," Laura explained. "He's a social guy, and he always likes to know what's going on."

Nancy watched as Mr. Jackson and his wife strolled toward the tent, shaking hands with friends along the way. At the same time, the fluttering pages of a magazine or catalog on the ground near Mr. Jackson's sports car caught her eye. Nancy leaned down to pick it up. A clothes catalog, she mused, and flipped idly through the pages.

Suddenly, she noticed a page where two large letters had been cut out. She caught her breath.

Had someone used this catalog to cut out letters for the kidnapping note about Morning Glory?

13

Dancing with Disaster

Clutching the catalog, Nancy peered at the address on it in the parking lot's dim light: Resident, 132 White Rock Road, Cold Spring, MD. Mr. Jackson lived on White Rock Road, she remembered.

Had he used this catalog to make the kidnapping note? Did this prove he was the culprit?

Her mind in a whirl, Nancy followed Laura and George into the tent. She looked around for Mr. Jackson and his wife, but already they'd been swallowed up by the crowd. The ball was in full swing. Around her, men in tuxedos and women in evening dresses chatted amiably. A band was playing jazz, and people were streaming onto the dance floor. There was a constant happy murmur of voices.

Mrs. Passano, in a sweeping emerald green silk gown, waved to the girls from the side of the tent. She was busily chatting with Mrs. Shaw, whose simple white dress showed off a strand of black pearls. "Alexa's here somewhere," Mrs. Passano announced to Laura.

Laura smiled and waved. "As if I cared where Alexa is," she muttered to Nancy.

The girls drifted over to a long side table to get soft drinks. Mark Plonsky stepped over to join them. Nancy had to admit he looked handsome in his black tuxedo.

"I've been waiting for you to come," he said. "Want to dance, George?"

"Yes, I'd like to," George said, smiling. She took his arm, and he swept her into the crowd of dancers.

"I hope George remembers that Mark's still a suspect," Nancy whispered to Laura. "He could be being nice to her so she'll take his side."

"If Mark's hiding Morning Glory," Laura declared, "it won't matter if he has George on his side—he'll still need to answer to me."

Just then a pleasant-looking curly-haired guy asked Laura to dance. Nancy threaded her way through the mingling groups of people, looking for Charles Jackson. He seemed to have disappeared, she thought, feeling frustrated.

Then she felt a tug on her arm. She pivoted in surprise. A familiar-looking young brown-haired guy pulled her onto the crowded dance floor. "I couldn't let a pretty girl like you stand around on the sidelines," he said. "I'm Duncan Burnet, by the way."

Nancy smiled, reasoning to herself that she might as well dance—Mr. Jackson might be out on the dance floor anyway. Hanging on to the rolled-up catalog, Nancy joined Duncan as the band played a rock tune. She danced—and furtively checked out the crowd—for what seemed like an eternity.

"Why don't you put down your magazine?" Duncan shouted above the loud music. "You've been holding it forever."

"I, uh, promised I'd lend it to a friend," Nancy said quickly.

At that moment she spotted Mr. Jackson at the far end of the tent. He was heading toward an opening in the tent wall—she had to follow him fast! "And I see him right now. Excuse me," she blurted out.

Apologizing as she jostled a couple of party guests, Nancy headed for the corner of the tent. But before she could catch up, Mr. Jackson had slipped out through the opening.

Nancy quickened her pace, and in a moment she'd caught up. Standing just inside the tent, she stuck her head carefully through the flap.

Outside in the balmy night, Mr. Jackson stood several feet away from the tent, talking to Peter

Greenbriar. Just then the band stopped playing, and Nancy could hear what they were saying.

"Mark Plonsky's been helping us more than he knows," Peter Greenbriar said. "I've been eavesdropping around here, and from everything I hear, Mill River's doomed. People will be scared of hunting with Mill River. They'll come to your hunt for sure."

"Good news, good news," Mr. Jackson replied heartily. "Though we still don't know for sure that Plonsky's behind all the sabotage. And was he the one who took Morning Glory?"

Peter Greenbriar said something that Nancy couldn't hear. As she strained to listen, she leaned against the side of the tent, which caused the flap to billow outward.

Mr. Jackson whirled around and saw Nancy. Scowling, he approached her, stopping less than a foot away. "Just what do you think you're doing, Miss Drew?" he demanded.

Nancy looked him straight in the eyes. "I'm a detective, Mr. Jackson," she explained, "and I'm investigating Morning Glory's disappearance and the hunt sabotage. I had reason to suspect you and Peter Greenbriar, and so I followed you over here."

"What!" Mr. Jackson growled. "On what grounds could you possibly suspect Peter and me?"

"Before you get so mad," Nancy said coolly, "I

want you to know that I don't suspect you any longer."

Mr. Jackson snorted. "Boy, am I relieved! And why, may I ask, have you let us off the hook?"

"Because I just overheard your conversation," Nancy explained. "It's obvious that you believe Mark Plonsky is behind the theft and the sabotage. You're as much in the dark as we are."

"You mean Plonsky *isn't* to blame?" Mr. Jackson asked. Slowly, he began to calm down. Nancy glanced at Peter Greenbriar, who grinned. He was obviously relieved that he wasn't being blamed.

"But I still have a couple of questions for you," Nancy said. She showed Mr. Jackson the clothing catalog. "Do you recognize this, by any chance?"

With a puzzled look, Mr. Jackson took the catalog from Nancy and studied the cut-up page. Then he flipped to the address on the back. "I don't recognize it," he said slowly, handing it back to Nancy. "It probably belongs to Alexa Shaw."

"What?" Nancy asked.

"The Shaws live at 132 White Rock Road," Mr. Jackson explained. "Our house is 128 White Rock Road."

The Shaws' driveway *was* down the road from the Jacksons', she remembered now. "But I found this catalog by your car door tonight," Nancy said. "Could the mail carrier have delivered it to your house by mistake?"

Mr. Jackson frowned. "I doubt it. My daughter, Lizzie, is good friends with Alexa. She probably borrowed the catalog from Alexa and left it in my car."

Nancy paused, organizing her thoughts. "Another thing," she went on. "Why are you and Peter Greenbriar gloating over Mill River's troubles?"

"You can hardly blame me," Mr. Jackson retorted. "Last time I checked, gloating wasn't illegal."

"It may not be illegal, but it's not very loyal." Nancy stared at the groom, who took several steps backward. "You work for the Passanos, but you're happy when their hunt has all these problems? It sounds to me like you've been spying on Mill River for Mr. Jackson."

"It's not that," Greenbriar mumbled. "I can explain."

"You don't have to tell her a thing, Peter!" Mr. Jackson said hotly.

"But I want to," the groom said, inching forward a step. "I want to set the record straight." He glanced tentatively at Mr. Jackson and Nancy. "Just like I told you," he said to Nancy, his expression earnest, "I came to Sky Meadow Farm because Mrs. Passano offered me more money. But soon after that, I learned that Mr. Jackson didn't get the top post at Mill River. It seemed mighty unfair. After all, he'd been at the hunt even longer than Mrs. Passano."

"Yes, but the hunt members voted in Mrs. Passano because the majority agreed with her," Nancy pointed out. "Many of the riders wanted to introduce a drag hunt. She's in favor of it—Mr. Jackson isn't."

"A drag hunt!" Mr. Jackson spat out scornfully. "That's just like fishing in a bathtub! I can't believe that anyone would think it's real sport."

Peter Greenbriar cleared his throat. "Please . . . I'd like to finish," he put in. "Anyway, I felt bad for Mr. Jackson trying to start up his new hunt, with no support from the community. You talk about loyalty, well . . ." The groom paused. "I worked for Mr. Jackson for twenty years. I couldn't stand by and let his new hunt fizzle. So all I did was listen around and let him know that Mill River was in a bad way. You can't blame me for that, can you?"

Nancy was amazed that neither man seemed to feel bad about spying on the Passanos. But she knew they'd never apologize, so she decided to wrap up the conversation. Looking at Peter Greenbriar, she asked, "Do you remember what kind of bit was on Lancelot's bridle when we brought it home from the Shaws' yesterday?"

Taken aback by the change of subject, the groom seemed genuinely befuddled. "No, I don't,

119

miss. But it must have been the curb. That's what Lancelot always takes."

"There was a snaffle on it this morning," Nancy told him.

"Really?" he said. "Well, I did take apart a bunch of bridles this morning to clean them. Maybe I mixed up the bits by mistake."

Nancy nodded. His explanation seemed reasonable. She was amazed to hear him confess to any mistake at all. "And what about the photograph of Morning Glory that I found in your drawer?" she asked. "Are you sure you'd never seen it before?"

"Well . . ." Greenbriar began. "If you have to know, I *did* find it on the floor under my desk, the night Dundee was poisoned. I stuck it in my drawer—I didn't know it was important. I thought I had dropped it from a file. But when you asked me about the photo later, I was scared you wouldn't believe me. I knew you were a detective and all, and I thought you already suspected me of poisoning Dundee. After all, I did mix up the buckets."

Nancy pursed her lips. She was irritated that he hadn't told her the whole story right away. Remembering that Greenbriar's desk had a large space underneath it, she wondered if the poisoner had hidden there, waiting for a chance to add the Taberol to the feed. Either Mark Plonsky or Alexa Shaw could have given Morning Glory's picture to an accomplice, who could have dropped it under the desk by mistake.

Turning to Mr. Jackson, Nancy asked, "Why did you have a coil of barbed wire in your Land Rover yesterday?"

"I'd gone out earlier that day to mend some fences in my cattle pasture," he explained, looking exasperated. "Anyone who owns a farm is going to have barbed wire. Is that all? I'm anxious to get back to the party." Without waiting for an answer, Mr. Jackson disappeared into the tent.

"You won't tell Mrs. Passano any of this?" Peter Greenbriar asked, obviously miserable.

"I'm afraid I'll have to," Nancy said. "For one thing, I'll need to explain why you and Mr. Jackson are no longer suspects. But you know, you should ask yourself where your real loyalty lies. Maybe you'd be happier going back to Mr. Jackson's, even if the salary is less."

Peter Greenbriar shrugged. "Maybe you're right."

Nancy didn't want to waste any more time questioning him. She needed to chase down Alexa, to see if the cut-up catalog was really hers.

Peter Greenbriar shuffled off toward the parking lot, and Nancy went inside the tent. She looked around but couldn't find Alexa. Nancy realized she hadn't seen the young woman all night long.

Just then Mrs. Passano rushed up to her, her

eyes wide with fright. "Nancy!" Mrs. Passano said, gasping for breath. "I've been looking all over for you. A man just delivered this telegram to me." She handed a crumpled-up yellow note to Nancy.

Her heart hammering, Nancy unfolded the paper and read the message: "Break up Mill River immediately. Grave danger awaits you on Opening Day!"

14

The Party's Over

Nancy looked at Mrs. Passano in horror. "Did you see who delivered this telegram?" she asked.

"It was delivered by a messenger from Southern Telegram," Mrs. Passano replied.

"Could I use your phone?" Nancy asked. Mrs. Passano led Nancy back into the office, and Nancy immediately called Southern Telegram. She gave the operator the reference number on the telegram. "I'd like to know who delivered this message, the time it was ordered, and who the sender was," she explained. "And if possible, please give me a physical description of the sender."

The operator came back on the line in a moment. "The telegram was ordered two hours ago from a Baltimore office that stays open late," he said. "It was a special express rush order. The man who delivered it is one of our regular employees. Unfortunately, we have no record of the sender, since he or she paid cash. The sales agent who took the order says she can't remember what the person looked like. So many telegrams go out each day."

Nancy thanked the man and hung up, feeling frustrated. She thought about her remaining two suspects. The brown glove she'd found could fit either a tall woman, like Alexa Shaw, or a fine-boned man, like Mark Plonsky. Mark couldn't have been in Baltimore two hours ago, she knew. It was nearly an hour's drive away, and he'd been at the ball when she arrived more than an hour ago. Could Alexa have ordered the telegram? Was she even at the ball?

Nancy told Mrs. Passano what the operator had said. Mrs. Passano frowned. "I'd better call together the other members of the hunt board to tell them about this telegram," she said. "Why don't you listen in, Nancy? We might need your advice."

Five minutes later they were sitting in the office with the board's four other members—Mr. Hathaway, the Burnet brothers, and a man named Mr. Tsao. Nancy realized he must be the father of Lili Tsao, the girl she'd talked to at the saddlery.

Mrs. Passano introduced Nancy and then showed the board members the telegram. After discussing it for a moment, they all decided that Mark Plonsky and the other activists must be behind it.

"Plonsky may be at the ball, pretending to be a nice guy," Mr. Hathaway said, "but one of his pals could have sent the telegram for him."

"At this point we don't have enough solid proof to formally accuse him," Mrs. Passano pointed out.

"Maggie, you're always the voice of reason," Mr. Hathaway said with a smile. "But I think you're dead wrong here. I'd say we had proof enough on the cub hunt, what with that silly fox setup. And now with Morning Glory missing . . ."

"We can't prove Mark Plonsky set up that fox," Mrs. Passano insisted. "Look, Laura and I want Morning Glory back more than anyone else does. But I still don't think we have grounds yet to accuse Mark of stealing him. As master of the hounds, I'm making that the final decision," Mrs. Passano said, her tone forceful. "What we have to decide now is what to do about Opening Day. Should we go on with it or not?"

"Absolutely!" Mr. Hathaway said, pounding a nearby desk with his fist. "We're not going to be swayed by terrorist tactics."

"I agree," Samuel Burnet said. "But why don't we announce the situation and let each rider decide whether or not to take the risk?"

"I agree," Mrs. Passano said. "Even if we disband the hunt, there's no guarantee we'll get Morning Glory back. I think we have to catch this crazy person—and maybe the hunt tomorrow will make him reveal himself. Let me make the announcement to the crowd before it gets too late and people start to go home."

The meeting broke up, and Nancy followed Mrs. Passano into the tent. Nancy quickly snatched a plate of fruit salad from the buffet. She'd been too busy to eat.

Just then the music stopped. "Ladies and gentlemen," Mrs. Passano announced from the band singer's microphone. "Please, may I have your attention." An immediate hush fell over the crowd.

"We have received word that there may be more sabotage on Opening Day tomorrow." Mrs. Passano paused, while a ripple of outrage spread throughout the group. When the room became quiet again, she went on. "We have no way of knowing for sure, but there could be even more danger than there was last Wednesday. Nevertheless, the board has voted to go on with the hunt tomorrow. We will not be scared off by these threats."

The crowd broke into applause. Mrs. Passano held up one hand to get their attention again. "We hunt officials plan to go out, but no one else should feel they have to. It's your decision. Whatever you decide, you know I'll understand."

As Mrs. Passano ended her speech, a buzz of whispering in the crowd swelled into rousing murmurs of support.

"I won't let anyone intimidate me into not riding to the hounds," Nancy heard a man say. She noticed that it was Mr. Zachary, the older man who'd helped George during the cub hunt. "On Wednesday," he went on, "we were taken by surprise. But now we're prepared for the fight!" He looked around the room defiantly.

"I don't like chasing foxes," Lili Tsao said, standing to Nancy's left. "I've always wanted us to switch to a drag hunt. But I intend to go out tomorrow. These blackmailers can't get their way!"

Whether they were for or against live fox hunting, the members seemed to agree on one thing: they couldn't let the saboteur win. Nancy was impressed with their spunk.

Just then, Nancy noticed a commotion in the crowd. Looking over, she saw Mark Plonsky elbowing his way through a cluster of people, an angry scowl on his face.

George appeared at Nancy's elbow. "Mark is furious," she told Nancy. "He's been getting dirty looks ever since Mrs. Passano made her speech, and a man over there just accused him of wrecking the hunt. He's totally insulted. He's going home."

"I don't blame him," Nancy said. But privately she wondered if Mark *had* come to the ball only to set up an alibi for sending the telegram. "By the way, George, have you seen Alexa?" Nancy went on.

But before George could answer, Mrs. Shaw joined them. "Hello, girls," she said cheerfully. "Alexa's home sick with a headache tonight."

How convenient, Nancy thought. Alexa always seemed to be missing when trouble struck the hunt.

"To tell you the truth, I hope she's too sick to hunt tomorrow," Mrs. Shaw chattered on. "Better a headache than a head injury."

"Isn't her horse lame, anyway?" George asked.

"Oh, yes, of course," Mrs. Shaw said. "So that makes it certain she won't ride. I'm sorry, but I *hate* the hunt. My husband died during one, you know." Her eyes flickered with sudden anger.

"I know," Nancy said. "I'm so sorry. But if you hate the hunt, then why did you come tonight?"

"In this area, if you don't go to events like these, you have no social life," Mrs. Shaw said. "Excuse me, girls, I have to say good night to some friends."

"Poor woman—I feel sorry for her," George said as Mrs. Shaw strolled off. "Laura says she's been under a lot of stress since her husband died."

The band played its last song, and people slowly

headed toward their cars. Nancy and George walked with Laura back to the car. On the way home, Laura seemed glum. "I'm so worried about Morning Glory," she said. "I understand my mom's decision to hunt tomorrow, but what if somebody does something terrible to my horse because of it?"

Nancy gave Laura a sympathetic smile. "I don't think anyone would dare hurt Morning Glory. And I agree with your mom—the hunt might flush out some important clues."

"Are you both hunting tomorrow?" Laura asked.

"Laura, I wish I could, for your sake," George said. "But I can't hunt, I just can't. Not until your mother changes it to a drag hunt. I had a long talk with Mark Plonsky tonight, and he only strengthened my feelings about saving foxes from being hunted."

"I agree with George about the foxes," Nancy told Laura. "But I'm worried about the danger to the riders. I feel sure the culprit will strike, and I'm determined to catch whoever it is before anyone gets hurt. So yes, Laura, you can count me in."

The next morning Nancy and Laura arrived at the clubhouse, where the hunt was meeting for Opening Day. They were on their horses when Mrs. Passano rode up to them on Trimble, looking regal in her scarlet coat. She had driven over before dawn with Grant Hathaway. "We wanted to patrol the countryside on horseback before the hunt went out," she explained.

"Did you find anything?" Nancy asked.

"No, but there's no way to be completely sure that we're safe." Mrs. Passano had dark circles under her eyes, but her spirits seemed upbeat. "We'll just have to do our best," she added gamely.

Laura, on Lancelot, trotted over to greet Isabel Hathaway and Lili Tsao. As Nancy had expected from the mood at the ball, there was a good turnout despite the threat. Mr. Hathaway and the Burnet brothers, in their scarlet coats, were tending to the hounds. The rest of the crowd, in formal fox-hunting attire—black riding jackets, tan breeches, and yellow vests—seemed eager to begin Opening Day. The horses looked beautiful, Nancy thought, each one brushed to a sheen.

Then, on the outskirts of the field, Nancy noticed Alexa Shaw warming up her horse. That was strange, Nancy thought. Wasn't Alexa's horse lame?

Nancy rode over to Alexa. "I'm glad to see your horse is better," Nancy told her.

"Oh, this isn't my horse," Alexa said. "I borrowed this guy at the last minute from Lizzie Jackson."

As Alexa pulled on the reins, bringing her horse

to a stop, Nancy glanced at her hands. That's odd, Nancy thought. Alexa was wearing a mismatched pair of gloves.

Suddenly, Nancy did a double take.

One of Alexa's gloves was a perfect match for the glove she'd found near the stuffed fox!

15

A-Hunting We Will Go

"Alexa," Nancy said, trying to sound casual, "did you by any chance lose a glove? I just noticed that yours don't exactly match."

"Can't you see?" Alexa joked. "I'm making a fashion statement. One black glove with elastic and one brown with Velcro."

"Are they yours?" Nancy pressed her.

"Well, if you must know," Alexa said huffily, "I couldn't find my gloves this morning. I grabbed these from my mother's drawer. I didn't even notice they didn't match." Then she added, "Don't tell her, though. She doesn't like me borrowing her things."

Nancy felt a split-second rush of insight. The brown glove with the Velcro closure belonged to Alexa's mother! Could that mean—

Swiftly, Nancy ran through her other clues. The

catalog, addressed to the Shaw household—Alexa had probably lent it to Lizzie Jackson *after* her mother had used it to make Morning Glory's note.

The photo of Morning Glory—Alexa must have had it from when she was hoping to buy him. And Mrs. Shaw could have found it among Alexa's things.

Nancy's mind kept clicking. What about the pitchfork and the telegram? Mrs. Shaw couldn't have sent the telegram, since she had been at the Hunt Ball all evening. And she'd been off delivering pies when the pitchfork was thrown. But what if she had an accomplice—someone who had helped her sabotage the hunt and steal Morning Glory?

Nancy frowned. Why would Mrs. Shaw do all this? Just to stop Alexa from hunting, so she wouldn't hurt herself? Or did she want to break up the hunt for revenge—because her husband had been killed riding in it?

Nancy asked Alexa, "Does your mother know you're out hunting today?"

"No way," Alexa grumbled. "Lizzie came through for me at the last minute. But Mom would have a fit if she knew. She's upset by all this sabotage stuff. She's a bundle of nerves about fox hunting, anyway."

At that moment Mrs. Passano blew the hunting horn. Alexa began to turn her horse toward the gathering hunt field. "Alexa, please—one more question," Nancy said. Alexa rolled her eyes impatiently, but Nancy went on. "Was Mark Plonsky over at your house the other day?"

"Not that I know of," Alexa replied, obviously taken aback. "We barely know him."

"Is there a dark-haired man who works at your farm?" Nancy pressed on. "A youngish guy, medium height?"

"That would be Eddie," Alexa replied. "He's been my mother's gardener ever since my dad died. But why all these questions? Let's get on with the hunt." With a light flick of her crop, Alexa urged her horse over toward the hunt field.

Hopscotch tossed her head with impatience, but Nancy held her back, thinking. This Eddie guy could have sent the telegram while Mrs. Shaw was at the ball, Nancy realized. And if that had been Eddie lurking around the Shaws' house two days ago, he could have thrown the pitchfork. He must have been spying on her and George, Nancy reasoned, and learned they were investigating.

And the photo—Mrs. Shaw might have given Morning Glory's picture to Eddie on the evening of the poisoning, Nancy considered. He wouldn't have known what Morning Glory looked like. But in the end, he hadn't used the photo because the horses' names were on the feed buckets.

The clues kept falling into place. Of course, Mrs. Shaw wouldn't want to hurt her own daughter, Nancy reasoned, so she must have set the cub hunt sabotage on a day when she knew Alexa wasn't riding.

Could Mrs. Shaw have purposely lamed Alexa's horse? Nancy felt chilled at the thought. But it was possible.

Now, Nancy mused, Opening Day was finally here. And Mrs. Shaw thought Alexa wasn't riding. Could she have decided the time was right for some serious sabotage?

Urging Hopscotch forward, Nancy quickly caught up with Mrs. Passano. "I'm acting on a hunch," Nancy explained. "I can't explain why, but I need your permission to ride ahead of the hunt."

"Nancy, I can't let you do that," Mrs. Passano protested. "You could get hurt!"

"I'll be careful," Nancy promised. "But it's better if I go alone. Once I've confirmed my suspicions, I'll come back for help." Until she had proof, she thought, she didn't want Mrs. Passano to know the worst about her best friend.

Mrs. Passano sighed. "Nancy, you're a hard girl to say no to when your mind's made up," she said.

"Thanks. I just need to know what direction you're heading in," Nancy told her.

"On Opening Day, we always have the same routine," Mrs. Passano said. "We trot over some fields in back of the clubhouse. We turn right into the woods after crossing the brook at the base of the Tsaos' farm. We usually pick up the fox's scent

135

along the trail that winds alongside the Mill River. After that, we go wherever the fox leads us."

"Got it!" Nancy said.

She leaned forward on Hopscotch, pressing her into a trot. Nancy scouted around for booby traps, but everything looked fine.

After several minutes Hopscotch came to a small brook with reeds growing on either side. This must be the Tsaos' brook, Nancy thought. The reeds would make a perfect place for a trap. She carefully guided Hopscotch over the water, breathing a sigh of relief once she was safely across.

Nancy and Hopscotch trotted into the woods. This place looks familiar, she thought, as she rode down a narrow trail. But what's that rushing sound?

In a moment the trail curved to the left, and Nancy found herself riding along the river. To her right, the current was swift and turbulent. No wonder the forest looks familiar, she thought—it's in the river valley not far from Mark Plonsky's house.

Nancy reined in Hopscotch for a moment, considering her next move. Mrs. Shaw must know the route for Opening Day, she mused. With the closely packed trees on one side and the swiftly moving river on the other, wouldn't this be an ideal danger zone?

Easing Hopscotch into a trot, Nancy glanced from left to right. Birds were singing cheerily, and sunlight slanted down through the trees. Everything seemed peaceful, yet Nancy had an uneasy feeling she wasn't alone.

At that moment the sun slipped behind a cloud, and the forest darkened. Up ahead, Nancy saw a bend in the trail. As they took the bend, Hopscotch suddenly stopped, shying to one side.

Nancy gasped. Another few inches, and they would have plummeted down the riverbank into the rushing water!

Nancy caught sight of two figures moving around a clearing twenty feet ahead. They were tying something onto a tree growing alongside the riverbank. What is going on? she wondered.

Just a few feet beyond the clearing, Nancy saw a large brown building with boarded-up windows and a rickety-looking door. The old mill, she realized. The mill wheel churned in the nearby waterfall, with a loud whooshing sound.

Just then, the clouds parted. Sunlight poured into the glade. Up ahead, Nancy saw a blinding flash of light, and the world went white.

As Nancy instinctively closed her eyes, Hopscotch reared up wildly. Nancy was thrown into the air and hit the ground with a sickening thud. Hopscotch bolted toward the trees.

Nancy lay on the ground, her right leg throbbing with pain from the fall. She looked up and saw a young man who fit the description of Eddie staring at her menacingly. He took a step toward her.

Then, in the middle of the glade, something flashed again. Strung across the glade from tree to tree was a row of aluminum pie plates. The dishes flashed as they reflected the sun.

If the hunt came by, there would be a catastrophe, Nancy realized. Horses and riders would be blinded for a moment. The horses would panic— right by the riverbank. Horses and riders could fall into the churning water!

Quickly, Nancy stood up, trying to ignore the searing pain in her leg. The young man moved threateningly toward her again. A woman was now coming across the glade. It was Mrs. Shaw!

Nancy called out to her. "Stop these dangerous tricks and return Morning Glory immediately, before someone gets hurt!"

"Hurt?" Mrs. Shaw shouted with a wild cackle. Her normally neat gray hair was tousled, and her khaki pants were streaked with mud. "What do you think this whole setup is for?"

She turned to the young man, her eyes flashing. "Eddie, let's get rid of this girl," she snarled. "First come, first served, I always say."

"The whole hunt club's onto you, Mrs. Shaw,"

Nancy bluffed. "If you hurt me, they'll know who did it."

"The hunt club!" Mrs. Shaw sneered. "They're all a bunch of fools. No—worse. Robbers!"

"What do you mean by 'robbers'?" Nancy asked, stalling for time. Little by little, she was edging toward the string of dishes, fingering a penknife in her pocket.

"They've robbed me," Mrs. Shaw declared. "Robbed me of my family—and my money." She scowled, then spat out, "My husband left money to the hunt when he died. Well, I won't let that stupid club get a cent! If Mill River breaks up, Cameron's money will revert to Alexa and me— the people who should have had it all in the first place!"

"But if you hurt me, you won't get a cent," Nancy told her. "You'll go to jail."

"But first I'll have my revenge!" Mrs. Shaw said in a shrill voice. "Go to it, Eddie. Get her! Let's not waste another minute."

Eddie lunged forward. With a surge of adrenaline, Nancy dashed quickly around him, toward the string that held up the shiny dishes.

But just as she reached it, Nancy's sore leg gave way, and she stumbled. In two steps, Eddie caught up with her, grabbing her from behind.

Eddie wrestled Nancy to the ground. He dragged her beyond the clearing to the river's edge.

With a sinking feeling, Nancy suddenly realized where they were—right next to the old mill!

Nancy felt herself being lifted. Eddie was about to throw her right into the rushing water! If she wasn't crushed on one of the rocks, she'd be pulled under the churning wheel of the mill!

16

Morning Glory's Best Moment

Just then Nancy heard a crashing sound. Eddie's arm faltered for a moment as he, too, looked toward the noise.

The door of the old mill was slightly ajar. Suddenly, a horse burst out, rearing up and flailing the air with its hooves.

It was Morning Glory!

Like a flash of lightning, Morning Glory raced toward Nancy and Eddie. In shock, Eddie dropped Nancy. She scrambled away, as Morning Glory nearly trampled Eddie in a headlong dash for freedom.

Then Nancy heard the hunting horn nearby. The hunt was approaching! The aluminum plates, she remembered. If she didn't cut them down immediately, horses would shy. And with the riverbank so close . . .

Trying her best to forget the pain in her leg, Nancy scrambled toward the string of dishes. In one swift motion, she took out her penknife, opened the blade, and sliced through the string. It fell just as the hounds rushed into the glade.

Grant Hathaway and the whippers-in were right on the hounds' heels. Mrs. Passano and the other riders quickly followed. They pulled up sharply in surprise as they took in the scene. Eddie was lying on the ground moaning, his ankle injured from Morning Glory's escape. Next to him, Mrs. Shaw was standing stone-faced, glaring at the astonished crowd.

"Nancy!" Mrs. Passano exclaimed. "Are you all right?"

"I'll be fine," Nancy said as she limped toward the hunt officials. She dreaded telling Mrs. Passano about her best friend.

"And, Mary Lou," Mrs. Passano went on, looking curiously at Mrs. Shaw. "What are you doing here?"

"Why don't I explain?" Nancy broke in, grabbing Mrs. Shaw by the arm in case she tried to escape. Quickly, Nancy told the riders that Mrs. Shaw had masterminded the hunt sabotage and the horsenapping. Astonished whispers rippled through the crowd.

"Yes, I'm the guilty one," Mrs. Shaw confessed, a defiant gleam in her eyes. "It's all my doing. And you know what? I have no regrets—not a one."

"Mary Lou!" Mrs. Passano gasped. "Why would you do such terrible things?"

"Too bad, Maggie," Mrs. Shaw said, "but the Mill River Hunt had to go. My husband spent all his time with it, and now Alexa was starting to do the same thing. Even you, my best friend, were consumed by it. There was nothing left for me." Her eyes blazed with sudden anger. "And the money!" she spat out. "Taking my money was the final straw."

"Whatever are you talking about, Mary Lou?" Grant Hathaway asked with a puzzled frown.

"You don't know about this yet," Mrs. Shaw said. "Cameron's estate won't be settled for another month. But he left one-third of his money in trust to the Mill River Hunt." She stared spitefully around the group of riders.

There was a shocked silence, then everyone started talking at once. Nancy remembered the letter that Mr. Shaw had written—about wanting to do what he could to preserve the local countryside. That's why he left his money to the hunt, she reasoned.

"I'm the executor of Cameron's estate," Mrs. Shaw went on, "so I knew firsthand about the terms. I kept the news from you as long as I could. But in another few weeks, you'd have learned about your little inheritance. Time was running out. So I hatched my brilliant scheme." Mrs. Shaw lifted her chin, challenging her audience to defy her.

"I don't understand," Mrs. Passano said. "Didn't he leave you and Alexa anything?"

"Well, according to Maryland law, he was legally obliged to leave a third to me and a third to Alexa," Mrs. Shaw admitted. "But I couldn't allow the hunt to get one penny! I hate Mill River! It stole Cameron away from me, even before it killed him." Mrs. Shaw broke down, tears streaming down her face.

Mrs. Passano quickly dismounted. She handed Trimble's reins to Laura to hold, then put her arm around her sobbing friend and tried to soothe her.

"You see, Maggie," Mrs. Shaw went on, finally getting control of herself, "Cameron's will stated that if the Mill River Hunt ever broke up, then that money would revert to me."

"So you schemed to make the hunt disband?" Mrs. Passano asked.

"Yes," Mrs. Shaw confessed. "And I paid Eddie to help me. All along, we threw suspicion on the animal activists. They sure made convenient scapegoats."

Mrs. Passano recoiled at her friend's words. Then she asked, "One thing I don't understand, Mary Lou. Dundee was poisoned—but the poison was meant for Morning Glory. Did you try to poison him? And why?"

"Well, it's not like I tried to kill him," Mrs.

144

Shaw said defensively. "I just wanted to make your most expensive horse sick—as a warning. But then Eddie botched it up," she continued. "I gave him a photo of Morning Glory, so Eddie could identify him. But he put the Taberol in the feed bucket instead of putting it in Morning Glory's stall."

Mrs. Passano looked puzzled. "But how did you think we'd make the connection between Morning Glory and the hunt?"

Mrs. Shaw looked disgusted. "Eddie was supposed to leave a note on Morning Glory's stall, but Peter didn't leave the barn long enough for him to do it. I must say, though, Eddie finally came through. He took Morning Glory from your pasture and led him straight to the old mill without a hitch."

"Excuse me," Grant Hathaway put in, "but I think that someone ought to go find Alexa and tell her what's happened. It would be terrible for her if she just stumbled upon this scene with no forewarning."

"I'll go, Dad," Isabel offered. "Alexa was on her way back to the clubhouse. She was having trouble with her horse. I'll go there."

"Alexa?" Mrs. Shaw said. "She wasn't hunting today. Her horse was lame."

Laura explained to Mrs. Shaw that Alexa had borrowed a hunter from Lizzie Jackson at the last minute. Mrs. Shaw looked shaken. "You mean—Alexa could have been hurt?"

"Mary Lou," Mrs. Passano broke in sternly, "many people could have been hurt."

Eddie, who had been lying quietly by the path, moaned in pain.

"I think we've talked enough for now," Mr. Hathaway said. "Maybe someone should go back to the clubhouse to call the police. I'd go, but I need to stay with the hounds."

Laura spoke up. "Mom, what about Mark Plonsky? He lives half a mile down the river. I'm sure he'd be glad to let you use his phone."

Mrs. Passano wheeled Trimble around. "I'll be back soon," she said, then trotted quickly away.

"But tell me, Mrs. Shaw," Laura went on in a tremulous voice, "what have you done with Morning Glory?"

Mrs. Shaw scowled and said nothing. Nancy tapped Laura's shoulder and pointed toward the forest.

Under a maple tree, Morning Glory was grazing contentedly on some underbrush.

With an ecstatic yelp, Laura slid off Lancelot. She handed him and Trimble over to Nancy, then ran through the trees, calling out Morning Glory's name. Morning Glory looked up at her and gave a whinny, then went back to munching grass. Totally delighted, Laura threw her arms around his neck.

After the police had taken away Mrs. Shaw and Eddie, some of the riders decided to continue the hunt—at least for a little while. "After all, it *is* Opening Day," Mrs. Passano said.

But a number of people, including Nancy and Laura, decided to return to the clubhouse, where the traditional hunt breakfast would be held after the hunt was finished.

On the way back, Nancy and Laura kept an eye out for Hopscotch. Nancy was now riding Lancelot, and Laura was riding Morning Glory bareback.

When they were almost at the trailer, they saw Isabel Hathaway riding toward them.

"Hopscotch was found near the clubhouse an hour ago," she said. "I put her in our trailer for the time being. She's fine there for now."

"How did Alexa react to the news about her mother?" Laura asked.

"She's totally devastated," Isabel said. "She's over at the Jacksons' now, with Lizzie. Lizzie and I will stick with her as long as she needs us."

After cooling down the horses and settling them in the trailers with a hay net, the three girls walked over to the clubhouse. A big buffet breakfast had been set up in the tent, and some riders were already there, sipping glasses of orange juice and steaming cups of coffee.

Just as Laura and Nancy sat down at a table,

George arrived with Mark Plonsky and the other activists. "Laura, Nancy, hi," George said, as she and Mark joined them. "Mark swung by the Passanos' and offered me a ride to the breakfast. He told me all about Mrs. Shaw. I can't believe it."

"Neither can I," Mark said, shaking his head. "When Mrs. Passano came by to call the police, she told me everything. I'm completely floored."

"I hope the hunt board will listen to you, Mark, now that they know you're not terrorizing them," George declared.

"You and me both," Mark said. Looking at Laura, he added, "When your mother was at my place, she told me she has a surprise announcement. She asked me to round up all the activists and bring them to the clubhouse this morning." He gestured toward the group of protesters milling around the buffet table. "I hope it's good news."

A short while later, Mrs. Passano arrived with the rest of the riders, all looking tired from their active morning. Grant Hathaway's scarlet coat was spattered with mud, and Mrs. Passano had a grass stain on her breeches. Nevertheless, they were both satisfied.

"We had a wonderful run after you guys left," Mrs. Passano said as she joined them. "Though needless to say, my mind was on Mary Lou." Her green eyes clouded over.

148

"I'm sorry, Mom," Laura said gently. "She was your good friend."

"Yes, but the real person to be sorry for is Alexa," Mrs. Passano pointed out. "I'll do whatever I can to help her."

For a moment, everyone was silent. Then Laura asked, "Mom, what's that stain on your breeches?"

"I took a tumble," Mrs. Passano explained with a chuckle. "Nothing serious. Trimble shied at the fox when it rushed out of a thicket."

"I'm happy you survived, Mrs. Passano," Mark said, with a tentative smile. "But what about the fox?"

"Oh, he ran away," Mrs. Passano told him. "The clever little fellow outsmarted the dogs. He ran down a stream, so they lost the scent."

"Way to go, fox," George said happily.

Soon, the riders all settled down to breakfast. A murmur of voices filled the tent, punctuated by the clatter of plates and occasional bursts of laughter. As everyone was finishing up, Mrs. Passano walked over to the bandstand.

She announced that with the money from the Shaw bequest, Mill River planned to buy up and protect as much farmland in the area as possible. That way, the countryside would remain unspoiled. The crowd broke into applause.

After a moment, Mrs. Passano raised her hand to

hush the group once more. "I have another announcement to make," she said. "As you all know, the subject of chasing live foxes has been a hot one recently. Some of you feel that the hunt should stay the same. Many others, though, have been pushing to introduce a drag hunt." Mrs. Passano glanced meaningfully at Mark as she spoke.

"The board has always been torn by this issue," she went on, "but I'm happy to say that we have finally come to a unanimous vote." She paused. The crowd listened in suspense. "Early this morning, while we were searching for sabotage traps on the trail, Grant and I huddled together with Duncan and Sam. We already knew that Robert Tsao had changed his mind and was now in favor of drag hunting. It took some convincing, but we finally won Grant—the stubborn old goat—over to our viewpoint. He promised to vote for a drag hunt if we could prove that the activists had nothing to do with the recent sabotage."

Mrs. Passano looked at Grant Hathaway, her eyes twinkling with amusement. Mr. Hathaway laughed heartily, then gave her a thumbs-up sign.

"The Mill River Hunt has hereby voted not to chase live foxes," Mrs. Passano said. "We are a drag hunt, from now on."

The audience burst into cheers, with a few boos and groans scattered around. Nancy was completely surprised, and pleased, by the announcement.

Mark stared, amazed, at Mrs. Passano. Then he jumped up, gave George an ecstatic grin, and joined his fellow activists, who were all slapping one another on the back in delight.

Soon, the activists wandered over to the hunt officials, and they all shook hands. Nancy watched as the two groups mingled congenially.

Finally, Mrs. Passano and Mark broke away from the group and returned to Nancy's table. "I can't thank you enough, Nancy, for getting to the bottom of the sabotage," Mrs. Passano began.

"And for finding Morning Glory," Laura chimed in. "If it hadn't been for you, we'd all be at the bottom of the river."

Nancy laughed. "I know how you all can thank me—invite me back for another visit."

"Even if it's hunting season?" Laura asked.

"Sure, I'll hunt again," Nancy said teasingly. "But only if the hunt's a *real* drag." She raised her orange juice glass, and they all clinked glasses in a toast. "To the fox—tallyho!"